BISHOP

BISHOP

PHANTOM OF ESPIONAGE

JIM TOGERSON

authorHOUSE®

AuthorHouse™
1663 Liberty Drive
Bloomington, IN 47403
www.authorhouse.com
Phone: 1 (800) 839-8640

Published by AuthorHouse 04/16/2015

ISBN: 978-1-5049-0667-8 (sc)
ISBN: 978-1-5049-0668-5 (e)

Library of Congress Control Number: 2015905768

Print information available on the last page.

CONTENTS

CHAPTER 1

A MIDDLE EASTERN GETAWAY

Present day. Eastern Pakistan on the Pakistan/India border. For the past five days John Smith had been held prisoner in a secret prison run by a suspected fanatical offshoot group of the Taliban. He was being held on suspicion of espionage and smuggling Afghan Freedom Fighters through the backdoor on the Indian border. At the far end of a long dark corridor, flickering lights and muffled screams haunted the cold, damp hallway. At the end of the hallway, behind a three inch thick steel door, John Smith was doing all that he could do to endure the random exchanges of torture being administered by five militant Jihad-extremist soldiers. When one wasn't giving Mr. Smith electric shock, another was hitting him with a baton. When one wasn't hitting him with a baton, they were working together to water-board him.

"Who are you working with?" Through broken English, one of them led the questioning. "Who are you working for?" Smith remained silent. "Tell us the names of those who are helping you bring the enemy into our country . . . Tell us and this will all be over."

Minutes passed like hours as Smith anticipated and endured the torture. "This isn't fun for me either, you know," the soldier said. The randomness and yet deliberate and focused torturing was almost tedious and painstaking for the soldiers due to Smith's will to remain focused and determined, but like any other man, Smith was human and had a breaking point.

Delirium was beginning to set in. Sudden intervals of unprompted laughter from Smith were interrupted by the soldiers as they dumped water onto his face, which was covered by a blood-stained towel, some Smith's . . . some from previous captives.

Finally, one of the men removed the towel. Through red and purple swollen eyes, Smith looked up at his captors and coughed up nearly a pint of water. "What day is this?" Smith asked. "What time is it?"

The soldier administering the water turned to look at his superior officer. The two exchanged whispers. By this time, only two guards were in the room with Smith. "The date is not important Mr. Smith, because this will be the final day of your life," the man in charge uttered.

"Well then I'd say that makes it pretty important to me, wouldn't you agree?" Smith replied.

As he leaned in, the superior officer looked at his watch and said, "Today, you died on October 14th." Just as the officer was spitting out the final syllable, Smith (who unnoticed by his captors, had dislocated his own thumbs and released himself from the handcuffs he was in) lashed the open end of the handcuffs into the superior officer's eye so deep that it punctured his brain. In the same lightning quick motion, Smith grabbed the six inch blade from the officer's belt and in an instant, flung the knife at the subordinate officer's throat, killing him nearly instantly. He stood above the soldier's lifeless body for a second and gazed down at him apathetically. After a moment or two, Smith reached down and removed the small blade from the soldier's throat.

He gently cracked open the door and peered outside. Although he could not see any guards, he knew he had to be extremely cautious because he realized that his vision was not up to par as a result of the beatings. As he left his dungeon, he knew that the easiest way out was to the left through the lightly guarded infirmary, but instead he made a deliberate right. He crept down the hallway to where the other cells were located. As he approached the cell block, he saw three armed guards.

Armed with only the six inch knife taken from the officer, Smith knew he was outgunned, literally. This was going to take precise timing. With a running start, Smith charged the nearest guard. Just before reaching him, Smith slid into the guard and threw his knife at the next nearest guard, skewering the side of his face. As he collided with the first guard, the guard lost control of his AK47 machine gun. Smith, like a Hall of Fame wide receiver, caught the machine gun in mid air and fired off three quick shots at the far, third guard and then smashed the side of the near guard's skull with the butt of the gun. Smith sprang to his feet and reached down to remove two grenades that were attached to the guard's vest. He began running with urgency down the hallway looking into each passing cell. He came to the second to the last cell and stopped. "Amir!"

"John? . . . John, is that you?" the man replied anxiously and nervously through muddled English. Smith shot open the cell lock and reached for Amir's hand.

"Come on, we're checking out of here."

Amir and Smith had been sharing a cell in that dungeon for the past five days, and in that time the two became considerably close under the circumstances. When he saw Smith standing at his cell door, Amir sprung from his bed like an eight year old boy springs from his bed on Christmas morning . . . Like when he was a young boy and came down stairs to find a brand new Gibson Melody Maker electric guitar on which he learned to play early era Beatles songs (his dad's favorites) in a matter of days.

Together, they raced through the prison. At every turn, more guards were arming themselves and joining the pursuit. Smith could see the way out through a back entrance reserved for high ranking officials. The problem, though, was the small military collective made up of five prison guards armed to the teeth defending the door. Smith grabbed Amir and pulled him down behind a stacked wall of barrels, filled with sanitized drinking water. "I seriously hope you have a plan for how we are leaving this place," Amir exclaimed.

Smith looked around the room. He saw two bright red fire extinguishers mounted on the wall. With bullets whizzing overhead, Smith grabbed the fire extinguishers and aimed them at the barricade. "You may want to take cover, Amir," he said. He looked down at Amir's brown leather belt and yanked it from his waist and secured the fire extinguishers to the top of a barrel.

Smith smashed off the nozzles of the extinguishers with the butt of the AK. Like missiles, they shot across the room, one hitting a guard, knocking him to the floor with a chest full of shattered ribs and the other crashing into the wall. After causing little impact to the wall, the standing guards turned and looked at Smith with a look on their faces wondering 'Really? That's all you got?' Smith just smiled back at the guards, holding up the pins to the grenades that he strapped to each make-shift rocket. Just as he smiled, a near deafening explosion knocked down the back wall killing all of the guards. Smith, still smiling, looked down at Amir for affirmation of what he just did.

"Amir? . . . Amir!" Amir was down in the fetal position covering his head. Smith grabbed Amir and the two ran past a splattering of gooey viscera and scattered body parts toward the open wall, outside and into one of the captor's jeeps. As the two fugitives drove away into the darkness, Amir said to John, "Thank you. Oh thank you John. How did you do that? How did you escape? John Smith, I am in your debt for life, good sir."

In a nonchalant way, Smith replied "That's quite all right Amir. You buy us some drinks and we'll call it even. And Amir, I should tell you, my name isn't John Smith, it's Bishop."

As the two men drove through the desert night, Bishop started thinking about what Amir knew. He couldn't wait any longer. After nearly forty minutes of driving through the moonlit desert, Bishop pulled over and said, "Amir, who hired you?" The look on Amir's face turned from gracious to nervous in an instant. "What was the money for?"

Amir didn't know what to say. He really did not know what the money was for, but Bishop was positive that Amir knew more than he was letting on. "The only thing I know is that it has to do with uranium," he said.

Uranium, one of the worst case scenarios that Bishop could envision. This stuff is raw materials for building a nuclear bomb. If someone is out there buying uranium on the black market, then that meant Bishop's reconnaissance just got a whole lot more important. And, it confirmed in Bishop's mind that he needed to be the man who would stop the creation of a nuclear threat. He understood at that moment why his superiors had re-established FALCON.

CHAPTER 2

FALCON

In the 1970s the former Soviet Union was seeking allies in new parts of the globe, primarily in the Middle East, while developing nuclear weapons at an alarming rate. Their inroads into oil rich Middle Eastern countries such as Libya, Iraq and Syria, the Soviet Union posed a major threat to the "Western World."

With great concern to putting an end to the seemingly growing Communist ideology pandemic amidst a Cold War expansion, western alliances United States and Great Britain felt an imminent threat was soon to be at their doorsteps. It was in this growing concern, that the Central Intelligence Agency and the National Security Agency created a top secret espionage program called Falcon. Lieutenant General Jonathan Striker of the United States Army and Special Agent of the CIA; Walter Green the Director of the CIA; and General William Banning, Director of the NSA, were the co-creators of Falcon, calling themselves "The Architects."

Falcon was designed to be completely off any government book. Just like the famed "James Bond," Falcon gave its agents a "license to kill," but maintained complete deniability from the U.S. government. If any member of Falcon was apprehended by a hostile country or faction, the United States disavowed any and all knowledge of them. As far as the U.S. was concerned, Falcon and its agents did not exist. Not even the President knew of the program. The culpability started and ended with the Architects.

Lt. Gen. Jonathan Striker of the United States Army had a clear vision for what Falcon was to become. He envisioned a program that would not supersede the top government agencies of the world in the public's perception, but it would surpass the best of the best in reality. And that reality was covert missions that the public would never know had ever taken place . . . political assassinations, drug cartel hits, the occasional prisoner of war extractions. This elite group were living ghosts, phantoms whose existence was to make high level world threats . . . disappear. Unlike the United States Navy Seals, the Army Rangers, the CIA, IMF, MI6 and all other top level covert groups, the one thing that separated Falcon from its peers was its total anonymity, not just anonymity for its agents, but anonymity as a whole. Falcon was completely unknown to anyone except the agents and the three directors.

1974, two years into the Falcon program, marked the first big mission. A Mexican drug cartel led by Jesus Emilio Santiago, also known as "El Rey", was beginning to take the Gulf Cartel to a whole new level of power, wealth and violence. The Gulf Cartel first began in the late 1920s and 30s, smuggling alcohol into the United States during Prohibition. Since that time, the Gulf Cartel had engaged in various petty crime activities such as gambling houses, prostitution and car theft. However, in the mid 1970s, the Cartel began a highly profitable drug and human trafficking business. The Cartel was quickly becoming the preeminent drug supplier to the United States and Europe.

As the Gulf Cartel was beginning to grow, the government of Mexico was facing difficult and dangerous decisions on how to handle the rising power. The money being generated by "El Rey's" drugs was estimated to be between forty-five and fifty-five billion dollars a year, (an equivalent of six percent of Mexico's yearly GDP) and at least twenty to thirty billion was presumed to be there on sight. Needless to say, those kinds of numbers created a little bit of a problem with getting the Mexican government to cooperate with outside law enforcement agencies. Though the government officials in Mexico didn't necessarily condone the drug industry; they did realize the fiscal impact it had on the country, which resulted in a "hands-off," approach to foreign governments that sought to eradicate the cartel's business.

Then there was the frightening escalation of violence being exhibited by the "El Rey" Cartel. He used any means available to him to force himself into a position of being the most powerful Cartel in Latin America . . . using car bombs and throwing dynamite into the homes of his competitors. There was also the fact that whoever did betray the Cartel would be abducted, tortured and hung in a public area by his or her own intestines. Sometimes, "El Rey" would even order the hanging and torturing of a family member of the person who betrayed the Cartel, just to show the people that he wasn't someone to mess with.

Furthermore, there also was the fact that "El Rey" was beginning to be perceived a little bit as a modern day Robin Hood of sorts. The Cartel was very generous to the local communities, giving out food every Sunday and sometimes even handfuls of cash, thus resulting in the people not disclosing his whereabouts.

Striker and the other brain-trust executives behind Falcon, all agreed that bringing down "El Rey" and the Gulf Cartel would be an excellent target to start with in this new endeavor, and retrieving any of the presumed billion dollars "El Rey" had would be a bonus as well. The very first team of Falcon agents consisted of eight highly trained military soldiers. Two agents were former Royal Marine Commandos in the British Special Services, two were former U.S. Army Rangers, and four were U.S. Army Special Forces, or "Green Berets." An expert group like this was surely the right combination of expert killing machines needed to take on a mission like this, once they all got past egos and "pissing contests" over who was the toughest.

All of the CIA intelligence information on the Cartel showed many civilians in and around "El Rey's" forty-thousand square foot compound and one thousand acre estate. The idea of simply dropping a few bombs onto the compound at first sounded like the easiest way to go, but the U.S. government feared too much public backlash from the Mexican government, who would not allow such a mission. Striker saw that the only way of getting "El Rey" would be to send in a team to assassinate him at close range.

3:00 A.M., the Falcon team was en route to the compound by way of the brand new UH-60 Black Hawk helicopter. The stealth mission was the first flight mission for the Black Hawk, as well as the Falcon team. As it sped through the early morning night air, the team did its final mental preparation for what was about to occur. Commanding officer of the mission, Special Forces Senior Sergeant James Franklin gave his team a final pep talk. "Just so you know, if any of you get shot . . . I will kill you."

The man was not exactly a wordsmith but the message nonetheless was clear. The Black Hawk hovered almost silently over the drop zone, a small clearing in the forest just outside of the compound. The team repelled down into the large natural copse of trees that surrounded the compound. Swiftly and quietly they made their way to the western wall which was at the rear of the compound. There they found the only guard tower that was on the exterior of the wall.

Using a grappling hook, Agent Rowe scaled the twenty-five foot tall tower. As he reached the top, he peered over the top to where two armed Cartel soldiers were keeping watch. Rowe quietly crept up behind the two soldiers and shot both simultaneously with two R7 medium velocity tranquilizer hand pistols. Whistling down below to the team that he had control over the tower, Rowe looked through his night vision goggles and surveyed the compound. Franklin, Pine, and the others made their way to the gate along the northern wall, as Smith traversed the southern guard tower wall. "Team 1 in position," Franklin whispered into his radio.

"Team 2 in position," Smith responded.

"All right let's check out the party, shall we?" Rowe relayed over his radio. "We've got two guards in the southern tower, Team 2."

"I'm on it Eagle," Smith said. Smith lifted himself quietly over the top of the guard tower wall. The two Cartel guards were standing shoulder to shoulder smoking cigarettes. Smith unsheathed two small blades he had concealed in his vest and approached the guards. "Southern tower is clear," Smith whispered into his radio as he removed his blades from the guards' throats. "Team 1 is clear for entry." Blood began to pool at his feet, which looked black in the night sky. The guards lay dying in a matter of seconds from severed Carotid arteries.

As Franklin heard the okay for entry, he placed a small amount of plastic explosive onto the gate; just enough to blow open the lock on the 15 foot tall double doors, but not enough to for too many people to hear. "Fire in the hole," he said. "Breach in 3 . . .2 . . .1." A quick BANG! flung open the gate. Six Cartel guards ran to the entrance. As they approached the gate, Rowe and Smith picked off the guards one by one from their garrisons. Rowe noticed one Cartel guard running towards the main house to seemingly sound an alarm.

"I don't think so, buddy," Rowe said to himself as he eyed down the lone guard through his rifle sight. Before the guard could reach the doorstep to the mansion, the muffled sound of a silenced sniper rifle quickly preceded the guard dropping like a sack of bricks. A single shot to the base of the guard's neck dropped him instantly. "Damn I'm good," he said to himself.

Franklin and his team sprinted for the entrance to the main house. Room by room, hallway by hallway Franklin and his team searched and secured the mansion. Surprisingly, they encountered little resistance. They quietly approached the master bedroom where "El Rey" was expected to be sleeping. Franklin held his team up at the doorstep. He looked up and down the door, inspecting it for a booby-trap. He motioned to Pine, who was the team's surveillance and technology expert, to check the room with a camera. Pine pulled out a fish eye lense camera that was at the end of a long thin cable that allowed him to look underneath the door. Through the receiving end, Franklin could clearly see "El Rey" asleep in his bed. Pine recoiled the camera and grabbed his assault rifle. With a raised hand, Franklin counted down from three. Upon reaching one, the door blasted open and before "El Rey" could figure out what was happening, Franklin and Smith both fired three quick shots. All six shots struck "El Rey" in the upper chest area and face, killing him instantly.

The team secured the rest of the compound, executing all remaining Cartel soldiers. When they finished searching all of the property, Franklin gave the order to "incinerate the place." As they went from room to room, building to building, Pine and Simpson, who were the team's demolition experts, strategically placed incendiary bombs that would turn the entire complex into ashes in what would seem like mere minutes.

As the team left the compound and reached their extraction point, a ravine a half mile away, Pine pulled out the remote detonator and gave a final word. "Damn . . . that sure is a lot of money we're about to burn."

"I know, I know" Franklin said sympathetically. "But that's all drug money, and blood money. There's no honorable way of rationalizing taking any of that money for ourselves. Hit it Pine."

Upon Franklin's orders, Pine flipped the switch that set the compound ablaze. In less than fifteen minutes, the entire complex was reduced to rubble and ash. They left no evidence of their presence. To anyone investigating, all they would conclude was that this was an accidental, out of control fire. Because his body was riddled with bullets, the team carried out "El Rey's" body and buried it in the nearby forest. Anyone would assume that his body was just consumed by the fire.

Falcon was a success. When the team arrived back in the States, they were greeted by one man, Lt. Gen. Striker. "Welcome back, men," he said as the team assembled in a small room adjacent to a large military air hanger. "Because of your efforts, the illegal drug trafficking into the United States will surely drop considerably. And not to mention, northern Mexico will now be a much safer place without that lunatic around."

No medals, no ribbons, no ticker-tape parades, all that the Falcon team received for their heroics was a handshake from their superior officer in the back office of some air-force hanger. However, that really didn't matter to this team. This team of individuals was chosen for their commitment to making the world a better, safer place, not making the front page of the newspapers.

Striker stood in the front of the room and pulled out a small metallic flask from his jacket. "A toast . . . to the Falcon group. You eight soldiers have just written the first chapter in what will become America's greatest anti-terrorism effort. From this day forward, Falcon will lead the way in covert military action. You men are shining examples of why we are, and will continue to be, the very best of the best." He took a quick swig and passed the flask to Franklin, who in turn passed it around the room. "You all go spend some time with your families. I'll contact you soon with your next mission." Striker left the room and as he left the office, he left the door open. The men began to shake each other's hands, congratulating themselves on a job well done and out of the corner of Pine's eye he saw something in the hangar.

"Hey guys," Pine said. "Come here. Take a look at this." They all got up and walked over to where Pine was standing. He was looking into the hangar with a look of bewilderment and excitement on his face. "Do you reckon those are for us?" Outside the room there were eight six person private jets waiting for the soldiers.

"Courtesy of good old Uncle Sam I guess," Franklin said. "I don't know who's paying for it . . . and right now, I don't care. I'll see you around boys." Franklin proudly strutted towards the jets. The pilot on the first plane stepped out of the cabin.

"Mr. Franklin, I'm your pilot, Charles. I'm already informed of where you will be going," he said. "Just watch your step coming onboard sir and we'll be taking off shortly." The rest of the group stood and watched Franklin board the plane and like school children, they raced toward the planes. After determining which plane was which, they all boarded and found that their bags had already been placed on board for them.

After five years, the missions for the Falcon group became more and more complex and important, assassinating Generals and rogue military commanders, and on two occasions, Presidents. Neither were Presidents of the United States, but of countries in a different hemisphere. Due to the rigorous demand of the missions, and the extremely high level of danger, some of the Falcon members were feeling that an end of their careers were coming sooner rather than later.

Five members of the first Falcon group, including Pine, Rowe and Smith were ready to hang up their combat boots after just seven years. After their last mission together, an execution of a North African dictator, they all met at their regular bar in Georgetown, Virginia.

"Gentlemen, I'm out," Pine said as he took a drink from his bottle of Coors Lite. "I know some us have been thinking about hanging 'em up for a while now, and for me, it's time. It's been a true honor serving next to you guys, a true honor."

"I'm out too," Smith said. "My girl is pregnant and it's time for me to actually grow up and be responsible. I'm gonna marry her and settle down."

One by one the group agreed that they were done fighting. The next morning, Franklin went to see Lt. Gen. Striker to inform him of their decision. Immediately after the conversation, Striker called the other leaders of Falcon, suggesting they should have an immediate meeting concerning the future of the organization.

After a long deliberation, the Falcon brain-trust came to the decision that the Falcon program, though it was successful, would come to an end. Too much money being pumped into the individual agencies and too much pride and arrogance that they could accomplish the same goals individually was the main reason for dismantling Falcon. A governmental "pissing match." Who could flex their covert prowess the biggest? CIA, MI6, FBI, NSA, they all individually felt they were the superior agency and could fight terrorism better than the "next guy." From that day forward in 1979, the U.S. and British intelligence agencies carried on as they always had before Falcon. They individually fought the "Cold War" and the war on terror, with all having the same common goal.

As the years passed, Franklin and Lt. Gen. Striker took the dismembering of Falcon the hardest. Striker stayed in the military for another ten years, never achieving the rank of General, then succumbing to a fatal heart attack one year shy of retirement.

After his retirement from the military at the ripe old age of 27, Franklin became a special advisor to the Los Angeles S.W.A.T. department.

The rest of the Falcon team enjoyed civilian life, while some continued life in the police force, and some just enjoyed the good life of retirement.

CHAPTER 3

THE BEGINNING

Bishop was a complicated man, and a complicated child as well, the only child of Sam and Darcy Bishop, who were both career driven people by nature. Darcy, a graduate of St. John's University, was a nurse at Saint Augustine Memorial Hospital in the Bronx. She worked the long hours of the graveyard shift so that she could be home to have breakfast with her son, and be there when he got home from school. Bishop's father, Sam, was a Captain for the New York City fire department.

When Bishop was nine years old, he discovered that he had a natural ability for solving puzzles, all kinds of puzzles. He started with a 100 piece jigsaw puzzle of the Statue of Liberty that he assembled in less than fifteen minutes. Later, he eventually was assembling 5,000 and 10,000 piece jigsaw puzzles in unbelievable speeds. At the age of twelve, his father bought him an electric guitar for Christmas, a Gibson Les Paul. It was at that moment that Bishop's life began.

Just like anything else Bishop pursued or attempted, he excelled at playing guitar. After playing his first note on that Christmas morning, he was playing hits by the Rolling Stones, Led Zeppelin, and Jimi Hendrix by Easter Sunday. And he wasn't just playing along with the melodies; he was playing all of the lead and rhythm parts flawlessly. When he was thirteen, he started his first band, The

Electric Three. It was Bishop on guitar, his neighborhood friend Charlie on bass, and Bishop's friend from school Marcus on drums. After figuring out their sound, The Electric Three started rehearsing five songs to play at their first gig.

The performance was at his father's firehouse. The department was celebrating its fiftieth year anniversary, and as a favor to Bishop's father, the Chief agreed to let his son's band be the entertainment. The band was a hit, and Bishop shined as the star of the night. In another moment of clarity in his life, Bishop knew right then and there that playing guitar was what he was born to do.

As a young teenager, Bishop quenched his thirst for knowledge, and his thirst for achievement, by focusing on his music. To somewhat of his parent's dismay, he spent almost all of his free time writing and practicing songs. The top priority of course was his schoolwork, but since just about every subject came so easily to him, he had his homework done everyday with ample time to practice on his guitar. He would listen to every type of guitar playing to learn new styles. Everyone from Jimi Hendrix and Led Zeppelin's Jimmy Page, to the old blues players like B.B. King and Buddy Guy.

When adolescent Bishop wasn't mastering his guitar, he was reading . . . about anything and everything. As he got older, he became more and more aware of the world he lived in. By the time he was sixteen, reading the New York Times cover to cover everyday became second nature to him. Still an avid guitar player, his aspirations for becoming a rock star had diminished some.

On a chilly autumn afternoon in 1999, fifteen year old Bishop was walking home from school. He was still two blocks away from his house, but he could hear the sirens. His heart raced. He knew . . . he knew something wasn't right. He dropped his advanced chemistry book and sprinted the final two blocks. The neighborhood streets were lined with Maple trees and the leaves were just starting to change color. The crisp air was stinging his lungs as he ran down the street.

"Please be wrong. Please be wrong," he said to himself. "Please."

His heart raced like a metronome set to the maximum. When he turned the corner his house was in sight. Three police cars, an ambulance and a paramedic truck were crowding the street. "No. No, no, no, no, No!" he exclaimed when he realized his worst fear was actually true. Three hundred and seventeen feet from her front door, Darcy Bishop was struck and killed by a hit and run driver as she was walking to work. She was one month away from her fortieth birthday.

By 2001, Bishop, who was now seventeen, going on eighteen, was fully immersed into world events and politics. Due to his innate need to excel and learn new things, he had become increasingly more compelled to do "his part" in the Middle Eastern conflict.

It was a brisk September morning. Bishop and his classmates were sitting down in their third period calculus class when the news came into the room by way of a crying school counselor. "Someone flew a plane into the World Trade Center!"

The entire day, Bishop and his friends consoled each other as they continued to hear the horrifying events that were unraveling some thirty minutes away. FDR said of December 7th 1941, "a date which will live in infamy." For Bishop and any young person at that time, September 11, 2001 become their "day of infamy."

"I want to join the Army. I want to defend my country," he said to his father. "Not only do I feel like it's the right thing to do, but . . . I just have this feeling that this is what I should do with my life."

His father sat across from him at the kitchen table. Like any parent, Sam was filled with concern and worriment for his only child. Sam was torn to say the least. "You know that both of your grandfathers were in the military, as was my brother. And you also know that because of this irregular heartbeat, whatever that is, I was rejected for service. I just want to know, are you making this decision for yourself or are you thinking that it's what I want you to do?"

"I'd be lying if I said I didn't think about that side of it, but honestly I've made this decision on my own terms. This is something that I personally feel compelled to do," Bishop replied. After another few hours, Bishop had the full support of his father. In sixteen days, on his twenty-first birthday, he was going to enlist into the United States Army.

The day that Bishop left for basic training, his father said something to him that Bishop would never forget. "Remember, I'm proud of you no matter what. If this doesn't work out, I'll always be proud of you. Life is short; you need to take advantage of the things in life you enjoy most. You can be so much in life. Being in the military doesn't have to be the only thing that defines you."

Bishop would always remember those words that his father said to him, because they were the last words that Bishop ever heard his father say. Two weeks later, while Bishop was asleep in his bunk in Fort Charles Louisiana, his Drill Sergeant woke him from his sleep. "Bishop . . . Bishop . . . wake up son. I have to speak to you."

The funeral was four days later. Over those four days all Bishop could think about was his Drill Sergeant telling him that his father had died. Cardiac arrest was what they told him, but Bishop couldn't help but feel that his father died of a broken heart. He knew that his father never got over his mother's passing, and now that Bishop had decided to leave, he felt guilty for breaking his father's heart. Whether that was true or not, the guilt with the passing of his father shaped Bishop's life forever.

At the funeral, Bishop saw a familiar face, a face he had not seen in almost a year. When the procession had ended, he approached the young woman he recognized. "Hello Mary, it's been a long time," he said.

"I'm so sorry about your Dad," she said. Mary Wilson was a friend of Bishop's from elementary school and into high school. Though they knew each other since the fifth grade, they became instant friends when Bishop intervened in a situation that could have been life threatening for Mary when they were in the ninth grade. One day after school, Mary was walking home and as she reached the busiest street corner on her route to her home she dropped one of her books into the street. Without looking, Mary stepped out into the street to retrieve her text book. Call it fate, call it right place right time, call it what you will, but at that very moment Bishop was approaching the same street corner. Because Mary was looking down to pick up the book, she wasn't looking up to see the speeding truck coming straight at her. In a moment of reaction, Bishop charged out and grabbed Mary, pulling her back onto the sidewalk. As the two stood there, Bishop holding her close in his arms, they looked into each other's eyes with fear and a little bit of excitement. Even though the moment could have ended disastrously, the two began to laugh.

"Come on, let's get some ice cream," Bishop said with a smile, quickly downplaying the event. The new friends went down the block to a local ice cream shop and sat and talked until the sun began to set. "Oh, wow, what time is it?" Bishop asked.

"Oh geez, it's 5:15," Mary replied.

"I should get home. I'll see you at school tomorrow?" Bishop asked.

"Yeah, see you at school," Mary said with a smile. The two parted ways and began a friendship that lasted the next two years. They were practically inseparable. Each day they walked to and from school together, talking and laughing about the day's events. It was Mary that helped Bishop get through the horrific pain that he endured when he lost his mother, and now three years later she was consoling him once again.

"It was nice what people said about your Dad," she said. "A lot of people really loved him . . . cared about him."

"Yeah, it was nice seeing a lot of his friends from the fire department again," he replied. He was practically a zombie. He was so consumed with grief and guilt that everything happening around him was blacked out and forgotten in a sort of haze. "Thanks for coming today. It means a lot to me. How are things in Baltimore?" Before the start of their senior year, Mary's father got a new job in Baltimore working in the shipyards. They promised each other they would keep in touch, but as their friendship resulted in so many other friendships, it slowly faded away.

"They're good. Things are good. I finally started that book I've been meaning to write," she said. "So I heard you joined the Army."

"Yeah, I'm in basic training right now. They let me come home for the funeral. I'm going back to Louisiana tomorrow morning," he replied with a certain level of disappointment. "I never thought I'd be doing this this soon, burying my father."

Mary quickly thought of everything and anything to talk about to change the subject. "Are you still playing music?"

"A little bit here and there. I haven't had a chance to really play since I've joined the military, but I'm still writing music," he replied.

Standing there talking to his old friend made him feel good again . . . Bishop suddenly opened his eyes. "God, has it been eight years?" he thought to himself. The memory of his father's funeral and seeing Mary again seemed like it was yesterday. Every time that Bishop needed to feel comfort, he would just close his eyes and revisit those times with Mary. It was those reflections that helped him get through the tough times in Basic Training and through all of the training exercises, but the times that it helped him the most were in his first few weeks in Iraq.

Bishop was lying in bed in his apartment that was located on the base where he was stationed. He was wakened by the memory of his father's funeral when suddenly his phone rang. "Bishop, report to the PX," his Staff Sergeant instructed him. "It's 10:30 at night. Why the heck do I have to report to the PX?" he thought to himself. He hung up the phone and left immediately to the Post Exchange. The Army Post Exchange is basically a supermarket/mini-mall where soldiers can purchase things from groceries to tennis shoes, so meeting at the PX at 10:30 at night seemed a little peculiar to Bishop.

When he drove up to the PX he found that the lights were off. He checked the front door and saw that it was open. Cautiously, he went inside. As he went inside, he looked around to see if anyone was there. "Hello? Staff Sergeant?"

A voice came out of the darkened room. "Corporal Bishop, my name is Paul Donald. I work for the Department of Justice," he said. A tall, middle aged man with graying brown hair stepped out from the shadows. Though it was dimly lit, Bishop could make out some basic features of Donald.

"Please excuse the secrecy. This meeting has to be kept confidential. I've been keeping track of your short career, and though it has been short, I must say that it is impressive. You've made top grades in all of your training and courses. You have progressed to the rank of Corporal in just under three years . . . What are your goals here in the Army son?"

Bishop was standing at attention as if he would for any other superior officer. He was listening to Donald recite Bishop's own military career status like a laundry list of minor accolades. "To protect and serve the United States to the very best of my abilities, sir," he said.

"Okay, Bishop, okay. Now why don't you tell me why you're really here? What you really want out of life. I've heard the 'Protect and serve' thing a million times," Donald responded.

"Well, as I'm sure you already know that many of my relatives have served. I guess part of me feels a family obligation to . . ."

Donald interrupted. "That's really why you're here? Because your father never got to serve? Are you here because you feel it's what He wanted? Come on Bishop; tell me something I don't know about you. Tell me something that makes me believe that you're different than the rest of our servicemen and women."

Bishop dropped his head and closed his eyes as if he were embarrassed by how he felt. "Ever since I was a kid, I've had this unexplainable desire to be better than everyone else at what ever I did. I just didn't want to be better than everyone else; I wanted to be the absolute best, without any doubt or question. And this wasn't just a desire to be better than any competitor I faced, I wanted to be better than myself at whatever I did, better than I was the previous attempt at whatever the challenge may be. In class, I found out who the smartest people were, what they scored on tests, and I wanted to out score them. And if someone scored 100%, I would ask the teacher what I could do for extra credit. You know it's . . . it's as if I have been searching my whole life for something to satisfy this craving, this desire, this yearning for something better; a yearning to make a difference in the world, in my own world and the world around me."

Donald felt a slight chill as he listened to Bishop. He finally found the soldier he was looking for. "Bishop, what if I could make that happen? What if I told you that there is an organization created by our government that would allow you to find the satisfaction you're looking for? I'm talking about a group that would establish real change in military covert operations. A group that would take on the most dangerous, impossible and controversial missions, missions that the U.S. government would say they had no part in, and at times condemn publicly."

Bishop stood there in the dark PX building listening to Donald's proposal. "He was right," Bishop thought. This was just the thing that Bishop had been searching for his whole life. Finally, he would have something that would not only challenge him physically, but challenge him emotionally and ethically as well. This would be a true battle of self-preservation and self-doubt. As he listened to more of what Donald was proposing, he became more and more interested. Top secret missions, espionage, assassinations, the reasons to join Paul Donald were just too many to disregard. "Okay, Mr. Donald, I'm in."

"I'll be in touch," Donald said. He then promptly turned and disappeared back into the shadows of the dark store. Bishop went back to his apartment and was filled with anticipation and excitement. He fell asleep that night feeling a sense of relief, relief knowing that maybe for the first time in his life he would feel like he was doing what he was meant to do.

The next day Bishop carried on with his normal daily job responsibilities, as if the conversation the night before had never taken place. He carried on with his life, for weeks, then months after that conversation and never heard back from Paul Donald. "Maybe he changed his mind. Maybe he found someone else," he thought. Then, after seven months of waiting, seven months of anticipation, Bishop received news from his commanding officer instructing him to report to the infirmary. "Infirmary?" he thought. "That must be it. First it was the PX, now it's the infirmary." When Bishop arrived at the infirmary he was greeted by someone he wasn't expecting . . . his physician.

"Please come in and have a seat Corporal," the doctor said. Bishop's heart began to race as he shut the door behind him and sat down in front of the doctor's desk. "So, as I was going over your last physical check up with the cardiologist, I noticed something that worried me. When we had you take those extra heart exams to see if there were any problems, well it turns out that you have an irregular heart beat. Normally, this sort of thing doesn't have to be much of an issue. However, because of your family medical history and the extent of this abnormality, I'm sorry to tell you that I have no choice but to advise your superiors to discharge you from military service."

Bishop could not believe what he was hearing. Everything he had done in his life until now was a waste of time, he felt. "What the hell now?" he thought. "What the hell am I supposed to do now?" Two weeks later, Bishop was officially out of the United States Army and without a clue of what to do with his life. After being discharged from the Army, he decided to go back home and start his life over again. He was now 26 and had his whole life in front of him.

CHAPTER 4

FIGHTER

When the plane began flying over the city and the Statue of Liberty was within site, Bishop began thinking about his life before the Army. He thought about how life seemed so simple then. He thought about the days of when he had a family, now he's left only with the memories of loving parents. "Welcome to JFK International Airport; thank you for flying with us and I hope it was pleasant experience," the captain of the airplane woke Bishop from his daydreaming. When he got there, the first thing he did was find an apartment in the Bronx. It was a very modest apartment to say the least, but it was what he could afford for the time being on his military pension. Being back in New York got him thinking about his parents and his childhood. It also got him thinking about Mary. When he last saw her, which was at his father's funeral, she mentioned that she was living in Baltimore and trying to become a writer.

The apartment he found was already semi-furnished with a bed, coffee table, a small kitchen table and an old couch that had certainly seen better days. The first night there, he spent most of the night trying to figure out if the constant ominous clicking sound was coming from within his apartment or the one next door. The following morning he went to get a bagel down the street and as he was crossing the street he saw an ice cream store. It was the same ice cream chain where he and Mary sat and talked for hours when they were in high school. Seeing the store triggered an emotion in Bishop, an emotion he had not felt in quite some time. He bought his everything bagel and hurried back home so he could try and figure out how to contact Mary.

He rummaged through some old papers and notebooks and found a number that didn't have a name written by it. He recognized the area code as being in the Baltimore area, so he knew it must be Mary's. "What are the odds that her family still lived there?" he thought. His hand shook as he dialed the number. A woman answered, "Hello?"

"Hello . . . is this the Wilson residence?" he asked.

"Yes it is. May I ask who's calling?" she responded.

Bishop suddenly sounded like a nervous teenager acting on his best behavior. "Yes ma'am, this is Kyle Bishop. I was a friend of Mary's in high school. Do you know where I can get a hold of her . . . or how I can get a hold of her?"

"Kyle, I remember you. How have you been hun? This is Mary's mom. I'm sorry about your father. Mary was very concerned about you."

"Thank you, I'm doing okay now," he said.

"Mary has an apartment in Arbutus, south of Baltimore," she said.

"Okay, I believe I know where that is."

"She will be so excited to see you again," Mary's mother said.

After hanging up, Bishop was even more nervous now knowing where Mary was. What would he say? What would they talk about? What kind of relationship did he want to have exactly? What if she was dating someone and things would be to awkward and difficult to handle having a friendship? He contemplated the whole night and finally decided on writing her a letter.

Dear Mary,

    It has been a long time since we have spoken and I am sorry for that. I really wish that I had handled our friendship differently . . . better. When you came to my father's funeral, it really meant a lot to me and I will be eternally grateful for that. I recently was discharged from the military and I am back in the Bronx starting my life over again. The apartment I am living in right now resembles something like, well if you could close your eyes and picture a really nice modern looking apartment with wonderful views and top of the line furniture . . . and then picture the exact opposite of that, that is what my apartment is like.

Right now, I'm living on my military pension but I hope to find work soon. I'm thinking about maybe going to school and joining the fire department. I hope that we can one day meet and catch up. I would love to hear from you and what you are doing now. I hope to hear from you soon.

Your friend,
Kyle

It was only three days after he landed in New York that he ran into old friends from high school. The same three friends from "Trivial Meaning," their band in high school. The band had broken up when Greg, the bass player, and his brother Steve, the drummer, moved to New Jersey their senior year. For a short time they tried to make it work, but after Bishop's mother had passed away, his heart wasn't really into playing. Now, Greg, Steve, Bishop and James, the lead guitarist, were all together again. Perhaps fate was intervening in Bishop's life once again.

For the next three weeks, the four newly rejoined friends practiced and rehearsed songs that Greg and Steve had already begun writing. The band started playing as if they had never parted. The chemistry among them was still there and as strong as it ever was. Song after song the four wrote and practiced. Every day, they gathered and practiced because they knew they had something special. They believed they could make it in an industry where so many dreamers and one hit wonders fell by the way side. As they got closer to the point where they felt confident enough to record a demo tape and try sending it to radio stations and music labels, they also started thinking of names for the band.

Still playing as an unnamed band, Greg and Steve secured their first live performance since high school. The Bronze Room was a small, hole in the wall club that had a maximum capacity of one hundred and ninety-five people. This was not exactly Madison Square Garden but it was a start for them. They were slated as the headlining band, playing behind two other unknown bands.

The first band to go on was actually quite good. By the end of the first band's set, the "crowd," (a word used very loosely to describe the scene that night,) was really cheering for them. The second artist to grace the stage that night was a solo artist who called himself, "Elvis with Love Handles." He was quite possibly the most entertaining performer that Bishop or the band had ever seen. "Elvis" sang mostly cover songs that he said were "meaningful gems that painted images of the trials and triumphs of my life."

This guy was about three-hundred and seventy-five pounds of McDonald's Big Macs and Burger King Whoppers. It was clear to say that "salad" was not in this guy's vocabulary; however it's quite possible this guy had sucked down a few hundred gallons of KFC macaroni salad in his day.

As he braved the expansive thirty feet from his seat to the stage, sweat began to bead and drip from his forehead like water droplets forming on a glass of water. The anticipation of his singing was building by the second in the silence before he began his first song. Will he even be able to finish singing his song? Will he have enough breath to finish? What song will he attempt? What kind of monumental, disastrous treat were Bishop and his band be in store to witness?

Finally, the music started. "Dream Weaver" by Gary Wright. "Oh boy, this will be painful to watch . . .," Bishop thought "and even more painful to listen to." I'm not making a knock against Gary Wright or "Dream Weaver" or anything. I mean it wasn't a bad song, but with that being said, the music started and when he began to sing, everyone collectively stopped and listened in awe.

He sang, and he sang, and he sang the hell out of that song, and he did it beautifully. He sang like an angel, they thought, an angel destined for early age cardiac arrest, but an angel none the less.

When "Elvis" had finished, Bishop and his band took the stage. Even with such a small crowd, Bishop felt like he was a star. Their first few songs were cover songs, but when they got comfortable on stage they played three songs they had written. Had it not been for one of the amplifiers giving off a bone chilling screech at the beginning of their set, the guys all felt that the night was a total success.

One day Bishop and Greg were sitting at Greg's house watching Star Wars and in a moment of not quite novel genius, they looked at each other, . . . thinking the exact same thing. With a combination of seeing Darth Vader on the screen and a shared affinity for KISS, they thought wearing masks and painting their faces on stage would be fun and a gimmick that had high potential of being a very profitable one. It had worked brilliantly for bands like KISS and the prospect of having the same kind of success was very enticing. Bishop decided on wearing a modified Darth Vader helmet that he could sing clearly out of for his first mask. The idea of masks would also prove invaluable to Bishop, who could keep a level of incognito in the public eye. Now, all the band needed was a name.

Over the following weeks, the band practiced and wrote music, fine tuning what they all hoped would become their dream come true. According to Bishop, their sound was a cross between RUSH and Metallica. During those early weeks of rehearsing, Bishop was at the same time writing Mary. In one of his letters, Bishop let Mary know about the idea of wearing the masks. She was one of the very few people who knew what the members of the band looked like. It was from one of her letters that the band got its inspiration for their name.

Dear Kyle,

> *Today I found myself wondering if we would ever be reunited. There are many things in life that are good and pure, but it is not that often that you are fortunate enough to get to have any of those things in your life. I cherish the moments right before I open my mailbox, anticipating a letter from you. I also notice that when I am thinking about you, I end up being completely scatter-brained and nothing comes out right. What do you do to me??? Anyway, the reason I started writing this letter was in response to your last letter in which you mentioned that you were feeling skeptical and losing hope for the success of the band. I wanted to remind*

you of how strong you are and how I believe in you. I believe
you can do absolutely anything. You're a fighter, just like
your dad was. He would be so proud to see you making
something of yourself, doing what you love.

With love,
Mary

It was just that fast. A simple, yet consequential blurb at the
end of a letter gave Bishop the idea. The new band, *"**Fighter**,"*
became an instant favorite in the local New York club and bar
scene. Overnight, they became a favorite of just about every 14 to
30 year old in all of the New York boroughs. After just two months
of playing nightly shows at some of the hottest venues in the city,
they were signed to one of the biggest rock and roll labels out there.
Just as quickly as their rise to local fame, they became nationally
popular after their first single, "You Make Me," hit the airwaves.
Bishop had become a bona fide rock star. Their second single, "Over
and Over," reached number eight on the charts in London. They
were quickly becoming the biggest band around.

Though the sudden success for Bishop was greatly appreciated
outwardly, internally it didn't seem to positively affect him at all.
He went for a walk near his old house in the Bronx, about five miles
from Yankee Stadium. It was early Autumn and the leaves on the
maple trees were already starting to change colors. The air was brisk,
but not cold enough to bother him. He just wanted to get away.

Soon, he found himself standing in front of the Bronx Zoo.
He paid the $20 to get in without even thinking about it. He just
wanted to get away. The immediate, distinct odor of the zoo, the
combination of a menagerie of live animals and feces, none of these
things bothered him. However, the moment that he came within
sight of a family, . . . a husband, a wife, a daughter in pigtails,
a son in a stroller, . . . and soon he was running for the nearest
restroom. He couldn't control the feeling of claustrophobia and
fear of commitment. He just wanted to get away.

CHAPTER 5

MISSION ONE

Nine months after their first single came out and they hit national fame, Fighter was getting ready to go on their first international tour. They were slated to perform a total of fifteen shows in England, Norway, Sweden, Finland, Denmark and Germany and if they sold out enough of those, they could join U2 in Spain as their opening act.

When their plane landed in London, the band was energized. Excitement pulsated through their veins. Bishop was humming "We Are the Champions" through the terminal when he stopped dead in his tracks. He turned completely white when he saw a familiar face waiting for him near the baggage pick up. It was Paul Donald. At first, Bishop thought that he was imagining it, but as he approached Donald, he realized that this was real. This was really happening.

It had been roughly a year since his encounter with Donald, but Bishop remembered it as if it had taken place last night. Bishop knew that this was no coincidence. He knew that Donald was there for Bishop. After a year of waiting, finally the moment Bishop was anticipating had arrived. But why now? Bishop knew that Donald must have known about his heart condition and that was ultimately the reason he had not heard back from him.

"Hello Bishop, it's good to see you again," Donald said as Bishop approached him. "I've been keeping track of your success. You've done well for yourself."

"I waited a long time to hear from you Mr. Donald," Bishop replied. "I didn't think that I ever would. What brings you to England?"

"Meet me at this address in one hour. We have some things we need to discuss," Donald said as he handed Bishop his business card with an address written on the back.

Bishop and the band picked up their luggage and took the limousine that was waiting for them, to the Ritz in London. After taking his bags to his room, Bishop snuck down through the lobby and hailed a cab and went to the address on the back of Donald's business card. "O'Malley's Pub" he read as the cab pulled up to his destination. He went inside and found Donald sitting alone in the back of the pub. He pulled up a chair and sat down across from him and asked "What am I doing here, Donald?"

"How did you feel when you were discharged from the Army, Bishop?" he asked.

"That was one of the hardest days of my life. Next to the passing of both of my parents, I couldn't tell you a more disappointing day I've had to endure," he replied.

"Do you remember what I told you about the organization I proposed to you? Do you remember when I said that the agents would be completely off the government books. Complete unknowns in the world of counter intelligence. Do you remember that?" Donald asked.

"Of course I remember. I remember everything about that conversation. I also remember you telling me that you would get back to me, and until today, that never happened," Bishop said.

"This organization needs to be completely secret. Everything about it needs to remain incognito, for lack of a better term. It's missions, it's agents, it's simple acknowledgement that it even exists by the United States government needs to be held secret for it to be successful. When you were making a name for yourself in the Army, you were exemplifying everything I was looking for in an agent to start this organization. Unfortunately, the fact that you were making a name for yourself posed a problem for us with regard to secrecy. We need soldiers to carry out missions that no one would ever expect, a true spy in every essence of the word. Like I said earlier, I've been keeping track of your success, Bishop. After we met that night in the PX, I set up the covert organization I was proposing to you.

This organization began decades ago, but now my superiors and I are reopening Falcon. Only this time, we're only going to use a few agents working alone as opposed to a military unit. All I needed to get it active were the agents. I needed you Bishop. So, I had your medical records altered. I altered them so that you would be discharged from military service. I needed you to be a civilian again, and when you achieved this new found fame, I thought that was the absolute perfect cover for you. Bishop, I'm here to offer you the job I offered to you back in the PX that night. I'm offering you a job to carry out top secret operations while you're living your public civilian life as a rock star . . . the perfect cover. Go be on tour, while at the same time you're helping us."

"If I didn't know any better, I'd say this whole idea sounds like movie . . . or a book, but who'd believe this idea?" Bishop said.

Bishop sat back in his chair and tried to play it off as if he were really contemplating the offer, but the truth is that all he was actually thinking was "It's about damn time." Bishop leaned forward and said to Donald, "When do I start?"

"I have a reconnaissance mission for you here in London. We have suspicion that a gentleman by the name of Wesley O'Conner is selling British intelligence to someone in Eastern Europe. We need you to trail O'Conner and find out who his contact is. That is all," Donald said.

It sounded simple enough for Bishop, just follow someone around. What the young twenty-six year old Bishop didn't know was that O'Conner had round the clock security protection. He was driven everywhere in one of three Mercedes S500s. In each car there were two fully armed guards. This guy traveled around with an entourage that could've protected the President of the United States. He didn't know who this guy was, but it was going to be an interesting challenge finding out.

Bishop returned back to his hotel and met with his tour manager and the band. They discussed the itinerary for their tour, as well as some guidelines and cultural rules they should follow while they were in Europe. After their meeting was done they all went their separate ways to sight-see and experience London. The show wasn't until the following night so they had about twenty hours to kill before they needed to be at the venue for sound check. As he left the hotel room, Bishop called Donald to get information on where O'Conner was going to be. Donald gave Bishop the address of O'Conner's private residence in London and told Bishop that he expected O'Conner to still be there.

Bishop went down-stairs and got into his car and drove to the address he was given. Just as he was pulling up to the home, the caravan of Mercedes' pulled out of the gate. He followed them to a private country club whose members included eleven members of the Royal family, Sting, and several other "who's who" of entertainment. "Jesus, is this a country club or Buckingham Palace?" he thought to himself.

The main building was just over two hundred years old and in some respects did indeed resemble a palace. Bishop thought that he was going to have to come up with some kind of ingenious rouse to get himself inside the club, but luckily for him as quickly as O'Conner arrived at the club, he was now leaving. Even more lucky for Bishop was that O'Conner was now accompanied by a second man. When they walked out of the club, O'Conner was in front of the second man and because of the angle of sight that Bishop had, he could not see the other man's face. He merely caught a brief look at the man's side profile from the chest down, which needless to say told him absolutely nothing. The two men got into the same Mercedes and drove off in the caravan. Bishop started his car, a BMW M5 on loan from the British government, and followed O'Conner. They drove west from downtown London until they came to Basingstoke, 50 miles from London. Bishop followed them to a communications building, Shinkiro Communications, a Japanese owned company. The cars parked in front of the building and the armed entourage escorted the two men inside.

Bishop knew that he couldn't afford to wait out front this time and try to get lucky twice. He parked his car across the street and went into the building. The lobby was a cold, vast space with only a single large desk with three people attending. One person appeared to be a receptionist and the other two were obvious security guards, dressed in the typical grey and black button up shirts with a security badge.

Bishop approached the desk cautiously, taking notice of where all three sets of hands were behind the desk. "Hello, can you tell me where I can find Mr. O'Conner's office? I'm late for an appointment." He had no idea if O'Conner had an office there, but he needed to get inside of the building some how. If the 'some how' was by force, Bishop was prepared to do so.

"I'm sorry, Mr. O'Conner isn't taking any appointments today," one of the security guards said. "You'll have to make an appointment with his secretary and come back another day."

Bishop didn't have time to con his way into the building; he needed to catch up to O'Conner. He went back out the front door and immediately went to the building's garage. Just as he turned the corner to check it out, he saw a delivery truck pull up to the toll booth barricading the entrance. Bishop ran and hopped into the bed of the truck that was crowded with vending machines destined for the building. He found a spot in between two of the machines so he could be out of sight as the truck passed the toll booth attendant.

Once inside the garage, Bishop hopped out of the still moving truck and went to the door of the building. He gently opened the door and looked inside. He saw no one. He then calmly and quickly went toward the lobby. He needed to try and figure out which floor O'Conner went to.

As he reached the lobby, across from the receptionist's desk he could see a list of names and room numbers on the wall. The names on the wall were in a considerably large font, but still he was too far away to clearly make out what it said. "Think, think," he said to himself. Just then it popped into his head. He pulled out his phone and used the camera's zoom to get a better glimpse at the names on the wall. Wesley O'Conner 301. "Thank you," Bishop thought to himself, he then turned around and pressed the elevator button. Unexpectedly, the chime from the elevator was noticeably loud. Bishop turned and looked toward the security, hoping they didn't hear it. Bishop stood there, his heart was racing with nervous anticipation. Finally, after what seemed like hours, the doors opened and Bishop proceeded to the third floor.

As the doors reopened, he saw names and photographs on the wall. As expected at a Japanese company, many of the names and faces on the wall were Japanese. However, there were a small handful of pictures and names that did not appear to be Japanese. One of those names he noticed was O'Conner's. Wesley O'Conner, Associate Vice President of Business Relations, he read. "What the hell is Shinkiro Communications, and what the hell does an Associate VP of Business Relations do?" Bishop thought to himself.

Bishop looked around the quiet room and could just barely hear a conversation coming from down the hall on his left. He quietly made his way toward the conversation and abruptly stopped when he saw O'Conner in the reflection of a mirror. Bishop squatted down behind an empty office cubical and listened to the conversation.

"I told you all of this last time, if you want that kind of information, then you are going to have to pay for it. This is not the typical defense budget information I've been getting you, this is high level, premium information . . . and I expect to be paid a premium price for it. Who else can get you this kind of intel.? Its simple supply and demand," O'Conner said. Bishop did not see the second man's face. He only caught a quick glimpse of the man from behind and he could barely hear his voice.

The second man Bishop could not positively identify by his voice because there was a slight whisper to the conversation, so Bishop could not clearly make out any distinct accent. However, because he could not clearly make out any distinct accent, he suspected that the man was an American. "I am prepared to double my normal payment for all of the schematic plans they have. Do you have those here with you?" the man asked.

Nervously, O'Conner glanced at his desk and stammered to reply "Um . . . uh . . . no, no I don't." Without even seeing O'Conner's face, Bishop knew he was lying and he assumed that the man he was speaking with also knew of his deception. After a brief silent pause, Bishop was startled by the sound of a muffled gunshot. Even though the assailant used a silencer, silencers do not really silence gunshots the way they are depicted in the movies.

Bishop thought to himself, "What were O'Conner's body guards doing? Why didn't they stop this guy from shooting O'Conner?" Since Bishop was just supposed to follow O'Conner and find out who his contact was, any motive to intervene was nil. Bishop did what he could to conceal himself from the unknown gunman. As he stayed crouched behind the cubical wall, he heard the man rummaging through papers in O'Conner's office.

"Look through there," the voice said. Bishop then realized that this guy, whoever he was, was the one in control of that entourage, not O'Conner. After roughly two minutes, the man left the office and walked past the cubical Bishop was in and then into the elevator. Bishop still could not get a clear glimpse of the man as he left the room, but he was now more than ever ready to get this guy.

When he felt like the coast was clear, Bishop got up and exited down the stairs and out the garage entrance. He quickly called Donald and reported what had just transpired. "Okay, come to O'Malley's Pub and I'll get on the phone with our guys in the States and try to figure out who this guy is."

Bishop made the hour drive back into London and gave his full account of what happened to Donald. When he was done, Bishop asked "So do we know who this guy is?"

Donald slouched back in his chair and said "No, we don't have the slightest idea. There's no reputable intelligence of an American dealing with O'Conner. From what you just told me, this guy must had been under the radar for quite some time. This doesn't sound like some small time, up and coming black market guy. This guy sounds like he's for real. Are you sure that the other man was an American?"

"I can't be positive . . . no," Bishop said.

The two men chatted for another twenty minutes before Bishop left to go get some rest before his show the next day.

For the next couple of years, Bishop successfully carried out numerous missions in Europe for Donald. During those few years, the unknown man never resurfaced on Bishop's or Donald's radar. One would say that the elusive mystery man was a driving force for Bishop in all of his subsequent missions. It was, in a philosophical sense, that driving force of pursuing the mystery man that got Bishop stuck in a Pakistani prison three years later.

CHAPTER 6

DAREDEVILS AND PSYCHOPATHS

When Bishop arrived back at his safe house in western India, he quickly got on the phone with his tour manager. "Where the hell are you?" his manager exclaimed. "You missed the show on Tuesday, and we gotta be on a train to Paris in ten hours . . . where the hell are you?" Needless to say, his manager was not happy with Bishop's sudden disappearance.

Fortunately, Bishop flew out of New York two weeks ahead of the band, giving himself some extra time to try and find out where the stolen enriched uranium he was supposed to be tracking out of Turkey was going, so he only missed one show. The trail led him into Pakistan, which was not particularly good news because Pakistan is no where near Poland, which is where his concert was. And then there was the other fact that Pakistan is not known to be the securest country in the world when it comes to potentially disastrous national security issues. When he got there, he trailed a courier that he suspected was transporting cash to a bomb maker in Multan, on the Indus River in eastern Pakistan.

"I'll be on a plane in an hour," he said in an apologetic voice. "I'll meet you guys in Paris. I'm really sorry Chuck. I had a family emergency. I left in such a hurry, that I left my bags at the hotel which had my cell phone. I'm sorry Chuck, but I'll be there."

Lying and deceiving had become almost second nature to Bishop. He himself could do it, and he had become a master of detecting it. I suppose it could be the result of losing both of his parents at a young age and he felt no moral obligation to confide any trust with anyone because everyone eventually leaves or dies. Or suppose that it was a result of covert military training, either way, it was a characteristic that Bishop wished he had never developed. Though he was becoming good at it, and it was beneficial to his career and at times his life, he felt it was bad for his soul, and he knew that he would one day have to decide to stop the lies. To live and potentially die in peace, or to live out his life and his death in oblivion in the eyes of his loved ones and by god . . . was a constant torment for Bishop.

After hanging up with his tour manager, Bishop had another line of questioning coming at him from Paul Donald. "So what happened Bishop? How did you end up in that prison? And who is this Amir guy, you brought with you?"

Bishop was still in his torn and tattered clothes that he had been wearing since he had been arrested. He wiped away some mud and blood from his forehead and said, "Amir is the courier I was tracking. The prison soldiers knew nothing, nor had anything to do with the uranium. They picked me up when they picked up Amir. He was trying to get through an area that had been blocked off by the Taliban militia. They started searching his car and found $75,000 cash, so they took him in on suspicion of terrorism against the 'regime.' I was directly behind him and when I saw them take him into custody, I took a chance and intervened. I couldn't let him get out of my site. If we lost him, we may never find out who's buying this uranium. I figured that if I could get myself locked up in the same prison, then I could get him out, and get him into our custody."

The reason seemed perfectly rational to Bishop, risking his life for intelligence that could possibly save the lives of millions. For Donald, it didn't just seem rational; it seemed that Bishop was merely doing his job, but poorly so. "You did bring him in relatively unharmed, I give you that, but what you did was borderline suicide, Bishop. We were completely in the dark with where you were. If you hadn't made it out on your own, we would have never found you. So the next time you want to do a reconnaissance mission, you better clear it with us first. Are we clear? . . . Are we clear?"

Bishop felt the stinging of disdain because he felt like what he did should be regarded as heroic and smart, not "borderline suicidal." "I guess I just can't get any respect around here," Bishop said under his breath.

"Don't you have a show to get to?" Donald asked antagonistically.

"Yeah . . . thanks for reminding me," Bishop replied sarcastically. When it was all said and done, the two men respected each other. Bishop knew that Donald was just concerned about Bishop, though he would never outwardly admit it. Bishop knew that Donald was really just worried, not mad like he presented himself to be.

Thirty minutes later, Bishop boarded a private jet that promptly flew him to Paris, where he met up with his band at the local arena where they were scheduled to perform. For lack of better terms, Bishop was lucky that all of the physical damage he endured was limited to his body and could be concealed by clothes. And although he was battered and bruised to the bone on his knees and feet and chest, he could hide it.

"Jesus, where the hell have you been?" Greg his bass player asked. He gave Bishop a friendly hug and then a playful smack to the groin. "We thought you were dead, man. We thought you might have checked into some hostel and never checked out, if you know what I mean?"

Just then, Steve and James walked up and saw Bishop. "Yeah, guys . . . I am really sorry about missing the show . . .," Bishop said, "and disappearing on you. I had a family emergency and I needed to fly back home. I left in such a hurry, that I left my cell phone at the hotel I was at. Again guys, really, truly, I am sorry."

The four had known each other for such a long time and were such close friends that, although they were pissed off that they had to cancel a show, they were not going to stay mad long enough to let this become a major issue. Ultimately, they were just glad to see that Bishop was okay. The band went to the stage for a rehearsal and without skipping a beat, they practiced their songs with perfect precision.

When they were finished with their rehearsal, Bishop invited his friends to a pre-show dinner. "Hey guys, dinner's on me. What do you say? James, I wanna hear about Susie and the baby." The gesture was received whole-heartedly and the four found a small diner near the arena and had dinner. They had ninety minutes to kill, and they took advantage of every second of it. They laughed together as they sat and ate while listening to James tell the story of how when he found out that his wife was pregnant, he literally fell off of his roof while attempting to hang Christmas lights. Together, they laughed all through dinner. When they finally finished, they headed back to the arena and performed one of the most amazing shows that Fighter had ever performed. The crowd was amazing and the whole vibe of the show was electric.

The dimly lit arena was charged with an electricity felt amongst the crowd and everyone else in the building. Hairs simultaneously stood on end across the crowd as the distinct electrical hum charged every ear as James plugged his guitar into the amplifier. The first note of the first song was received by a roar of cheers. For two-thirds of the song, it mattered not if they were even playing at all. All that mattered to the adoring fans, was that they were there in person, in the presence of their favorite band. A release, an escape from reality for ninety minutes from whatever mundane or trivial, arduous or depressing, pleasant or normal lives they had and for Bishop, it was no different. He too relished in the relief he felt while performing. For him, it was an escape of the dark reality that he lived in his other life-a life full of death.

When they finished, the roaring 21,000 fans chanted "Encore! Encore! Encore!" The band returned to the stage after a quick break and continued to play an additional thirty minutes of cover songs and some of their own material.

When the show was over the band hopped into two black SUV's and drove off to their hotel, Bishop and guitarist James in one, Greg and Steve in the other. They were still amped up from the performance as they drove down the streets of downtown Berlin. "Hell of a show tonight, man," Bishop said. "Could you believe how loud the crowd got?"

"It felt a lot like our first major show. Remember that? When we opened for U2?" James asked.

"Man, how could I forget? What did they say the attendance was . . . eighty, eighty-five thousand? That was by far the craziest experience I've had on stage. Now THAT crowd was electric," Bishop said. "Day after tomorrow, Manchester." The two reminisced for the rest of their short ride back to the hotel. When they arrived, there was a small crowd of fans congregating out front. No one's really sure how fans find them, but Bishop had always assumed that sometimes people from the hotels leak information to paparazzi.

The drivers of the SUVs pulled into the underground car garage to the hotel to avoid the adoring fans. When they exited their vehicles, Bishop, the always astute individual, noticed Donald waiting for him in the garage. The band went in and Bishop stayed behind to make a quick call, or at least that is what he told his friends.

"This better be important Donald. Do you have any idea how exhausted I am?"

"The mystery man has resurfaced," Donald said. That one simple non-descript sentence said everything. "We've followed a trail of large sums of cash deposits to a bank in London. The account raised suspicion to the manager when they received two wire transfers of a half million pounds in the same day. The only reason we know anything about it, is because the law states that if a bank dealing with any U.S. business, must report any transactions greater than $10,000 to the Department of Treasury. The transfers were coming from a bank in Italy, but they found that the account originated in the United States."

"What's the name on the account?" Bishop asked.

"Jefferson Clark," Donald said. "From what we found out, he's an oil tycoon located in Louisiana. Right now, we've got very little on him aside from what you can read in Forbes or the Wall Street Journal. This guy seems to be legit, but some of his transactions that we have confirmed coincide with some payments we have tracked or apprehended. We did confirm a payment made from Clark's bank in London to a bank in Damascus."

"Syria?" Bishop replied. "Can't these guys pick more enjoyable places to hide their money, like the Bahamas, . . . you know, like a politician would do?"

"Now, the recipient we have not been able to identify. All we do know is that Clark made a deposit of $75,000 to that bank ten days ago. Does that amount ring any bells for you?" Donald said.

"$75,000 was the amount Amir had with him in Pakistan," Bishop said.

Donald suggested that they may need some local help from people there in Europe. "So we know that Clark is dirty, we just don't know what he's up to. Even though it's pretty clear that the seventy-five grand on the courier came from Clark, we have no way of absolutely proving it. I want you to talk to some of your contacts here in Europe . . . see what Interpol has on this guy."

"I know who to talk to," Bishop replied. After discussing their revelation about Jefferson Clark, Donald gave Bishop a present, a symbolic gesture of the good work he was doing. "Glock 19," he said. "Thank you Paul." The new handgun would go perfectly with his military issued Beretta M9. In this line of work, having a small firearm that you could easily conceal was crucial, and to Bishop, having two was even better.

The two parted ways and Bishop went up to his hotel room. The next morning, they boarded a train from Paris to Berlin. Bishop decided to keep a daily, detailed journal to help him "deal" with or address his conflicted conscience.

Saturday,

    It was my first time to Berlin. We took the Metro from Paris this morning. The band and I each had our own cabins which were in a private part of the train. Our manager reserved the secluded rooms for us in an effort to give us privacy from people on the train; however it was evident that no one on the train could care less about us. After ten minutes, I left my cabin and ventured through the train. I wanted to mingle. The first woman I found sitting alone was an attractive girl, early twenties with a dirty blonde pixie cut. Normally, that doesn't do it for me but on some girls it looks good and this girl was pulling that look off. I asked her if I could sit down, assuming but mostly hoping that she spoke English, or at the very least understood well enough for me to successfully hit on her. She told me she was from Prague and she was in Paris visiting friends at University and now she was on her way back home. I asked her what she thought of Paris. She ignored my question and asked me if I wanted to "shroom". The idea of viewing the world around me through a different set of eyes for a few hours seemed like just the thing I needed at the time. We both ate about three, possibly four grams each. We made out in the women's bathroom until the man on the train checking passenger tickets knocked on our door. We exited the bathroom and went our own ways. Nearly an hour later I was sitting in my cabin, listening to Pink Floyd's "Shine On You Crazy Diamond" to help me stay relaxed through my "trip," when James came into my room. I'm not even sure how long he was sitting there in front of me before I realized that he was there, but when I did notice him, he had an aqua colored glowing aura all around him which was crowned with a brilliant violet halo above him. I think the drugs had kicked in. In that moment he could've been, Buddha, Vishnu, Allah, Thor, The Easter Bunny, Richard Nixon or Christ himself. The temptation was all the same to me. I wanted to crack him open and eat his gooey chocolate center before he flew away on his mysterious flying watermelon.

Bishop and Fighter arrived in Berlin later that night. The long train ride allowed Bishop to come back down from his trip on mushrooms. The city was lit up and the streets were crowded and crawling with people. One hundred thousand, twentieth century raver hippies filled the streets in preparation for Love Fest.

Seeing the thousands of happy, care-free, "love-all" people in the parade, Bishop felt depressed. He began reflecting on his life and the emptiness he felt. Later in his hotel room, he wrote in his journal.

Monday,

I walked alone all day in the crowds. It took no more than an hour before realizing that, despite being surrounded by scores of people, I was still alone. I could not, nor would I EVER be able to connect with any of them. Can a person be desolate? If my feelings and emotions are so barren and empty, am I really no different than a desert wasteland where nothing grows? No one visits or stays, only death.

Bishop woke in his hotel bed feeling oddly pleasant. Oddly pleasant because he didn't' feel the overwhelming feeling of isolation and depression. Light flickered and danced on his face like a luminescent ballet. The air conditioner was blowing down against the vertical blinds, causing the rising sunlight to shimmer through in an almost melodic pattern.

It was the next morning, but for some reason it felt like days, possibly weeks since his lamentation of his life just the night before. Fighter had one more show that night in Berlin, before they were off to Manchester. The Berlin show was just as electrifying as last night's Paris show, and Bishop relished in every moment of that show as well.

CHAPTER 7

A LITTLE HELP FROM MY FRIENDS

The room was filled with mounted animal "trophies," lions from Africa, seven different species of bear from all over the world, including a polar bear which has been declared illegal, rhinos, hyenas, and wild boars, along with countless other trophies that completed the menagerie of once living wild beasts. He was a man with a taste for the finer things in life and an obvious disregard for rules as long as he could benefit from it. He would do whatever it took to win, victory at all costs. "I will defeat you. You are no match for me." A woman, presumably the man's wife, but possibly secretary, entered the room.

"Harold, Mr. Bishop is here to see you," she said.

"Thank you Sally. Show him to the kitchen?" The man stood up from the table where he had resided over a chess board. "We'll finish this later," he said as he looked down at his seven year old grandson.

"Whatever, old man," the grandson retorted. "You're going down."

Harold Jenkins, a stocky middle aged gentleman from Manchester, England, was a career investigator for Interpol. Now retired, Jenkins spent his time hunting big game animals and beating his grandson in otherwise trivial board games.

"Bishop, it's good to see you again!"

"Harold, good to see you as well," Bishop replied. The two men embraced in a friendly hug which quickly turned into a reciprocal "pat down," which showed evidence that despite their three plus year friendship, neither one trusted the other. Jenkins was one of the few living people on the planet who knew Bishop's true identity as a covert spy. Together, Bishop and Jenkins worked on assassinating several notorious eastern European characters like Ivan Stonovich, a suspected arms dealer specializing in chemical weapons.

"Well now that that's out of the way, what can I do for ya Bishop?"

"Tell me about Jefferson Carter," Bishop inquired.

"The oil tycoon? What do you want to know?" Jenkins replied.

"Don't play coy with me Harold. What does Interpol have on him?"

Jenkins knew he wasn't going to able to give Bishop the standard rhetoric. He was going to have to tell him something. "Look Bishop, even if I *were* able to give you any intel., we just don't have anything. All we know is that he has been hiding a large portion of his assets in an Italian Bank that has close ties to the Vatican Bank. Now we've looked into it, but everything always comes in a nice, clean dead-end. The guy smells fishy, but when we scratch the surface the guy comes up clean."

"The Vatican?" Bishop replied. "Who does Carter know in the Vatican?"

"You got me," Jenkins said. "We've been trying to figure that one out for six weeks . . . So Bishop, are you here just for Carter?" Jenkins, as always, had ulterior motives, so he assumed that **everyone** has ulterior motives. Jenkins, the physical embodiment of faithlessness in humanity, but was never one to shy away from friendly gratuities.

"Well, we are on tour right now. We've got a show tomorrow night in Manchester," Bishop replied.

"So uh . . . any chance you can get my niece and her husband tickets to the show? I was supposed to take them to Italy last month but I had business here to attend to. They would love it and it would save my arse a little bit Bishop," he pleaded.

"Sure, no problem. I'll take care of it. Just tell them that I'll leave two tickets at the will call, for them, or I guess you guys call it box office." Bishop grabbed a bottle of beer from the ice box as he left the kitchen. "And cut back on the sweets . . . you're starting to look like Elvis right before he croaked," he said playfully.

After leaving Jenkins' house, Bishop got on the phone with Donald and had him arrange a flight to Rome that night. He would have until 6:00 pm the next day before he needed to be back in London for tomorrow night's concert. The trip to Rome wouldn't take more than a couple of hours Bishop felt. Talk to the Bank in Vatican City and try to find out as much as he could about Jefferson Carter . . . three, four hours tops.

As Bishop left Jenkins' house, he noticed a car down the street with tinted windows and two men sitting in the front seat. Without as much as turning his head to look, Bishop could see that the car had no front license plate and the two men both were wearing sunglasses on a day in which there wasn't very much sun. Someone was following him.

Bishop got into his BMW M5 and started driving toward the airport. He immediately noticed the other car starting to follow him. Bishop saw a street that was undergoing construction and made an abrupt turn and began to speed off. In his rearview mirror he saw the the pursuing vehicle turn the corner and speed up behind him. He could now make out that the other car was a Mercedes, just like one of the ones in O'Conner's caravan, just like your stereotypical vehicle of choice by every movie henchman in Europe.

The cars began swerving in and out of traffic. They were reaching speeds of over 90 mph. Quickly, they were approaching downtown Manchester. Pedestrians jumped out of crosswalks, dropping their mocha frappuccinos and breakfast scones, as they sped through intersections. Gunshots started blasting through the air. Bishop did not seem to be too concerned until three bullets shattered his rear window. From the corner of his eye, Bishop saw a construction scaffold on the exterior of a building near the upcoming intersection. He pulled his emergency brake and turned the wheel hard to the left. The car began to spin like a top as it moved toward the scaffold. With tremendous force, the car's right rear end whipped around and struck the support poles of the scaffold and launched the metal beams and wooden planks directly at the pursuing Mercedes. The flying support structure smashed into the windshield. The poles flew into the car like javelins.

The crash was incredible, Bishop, the ever cool and collected professional that he is, drove off as if nothing had happened. He drove maybe two blocks before he realized just how close he came to dying. He looked to his left and saw a bullet hole in the passenger head rest. The possibility of being shot in the back of the head was suddenly very real to Bishop.

He made it to the airport where he was supposed to be boarding a private plane to Rome. When he pulled up to a secluded tarmac, he parked his car in front of a gate that was being monitored by a young man who worked for the airport. Bishop tossed the keys to the young man as he passed by. "Here you go kid; have fun with her . . ." Bishop said, "She may need a little tune up though." The young man was ecstatic and shocked at the gift. He jumped out of his seat and ran toward the car. His heart sank when he saw the driver's side of the car that was completely dented, scratched and just about devoid of paint. He almost wanted to cry as he assessed the damage from the front to the back, then when he reached the rear of the car to discover bullet holes and a blown out rear window, he truly began to weep.

Bishop boarded the plane and tried his best to relax and enjoy the flight but the adrenaline pumping through his veins was making that difficult. After the plane had taken flight, he got up and went into the bathroom to splash some cold water on his face. As he stood there in front of the mirror, he became disturbed because he was having trouble recognizing the face in the reflection. The six foot one inch, brown haired, blue eyed man staring back at him was almost unrecognizable to him. The strong jaw line, slightly hidden by stubble, that he shared with his father, was still there. However, for some reason, Bishop was having trouble seeing the resemblance. The person now in the mirror was more of a stranger to Bishop than a familiar face.

When he first decided to accept this job, Bishop felt like it could be an opportunity to forget some of the things in his past. However, now just twenty-seven years old, Bishop realized his wishful thinking had become somewhat of a curse. Not only was he beginning to forget his past, but he was beginning to forget who he was as a man.

Thursday,

> *Today I found myself staring at a stranger for several minutes, wondering who this person was. Why was he staring at me? Although he looked familiar to me, I could not conjure up a name and that is when I became frightened. The stranger's face turned ghostly pale and my heart began to race again, even faster than it was when I was fleeing the guys in the Mercedes. That is when I realized the man's face was my own and I didn't recognize it. I've probably looked at my face in the mirror a hundred thousand times but this time, this time I didn't see me. What is happening to me? Who am I becoming? Am I becoming someone else, or am I just losing myself?*

The plane landed in Rome at 9:30 pm local time which meant that Bishop had roughly twenty-one hours to find out what he could about Carter. At 9:30 pm the banks were definitely closed, so Bishop went to the regular hotel he stayed at whenever he needed to go to Rome on Falcon business. He checked in under his regular alias he used while in Rome, William Asher, and went up to his room. When he got there, he found a bottle of Barolo Monfortino, an Italian Red wine that retails around $300 a bottle and up, a nice gesture to all of the hotel's regular and most important guests. Still exhausted from the afternoon's adventure, Bishop popped open the bottle, poured himself a full glass, and relaxed in one of the room's large, plush, heavily cushioned chairs. He positioned the chair looking out toward the room's balcony and watched the city lights below.

When Bishop awoke, he felt a tight restraint on his arms. He tried to lift them, but the harder he tried the more he realized that he could not move. He was now fully awake and as he looked down toward his arms, he saw that someone had tied his arms down to the bed. His arms at the wrists, his legs at the ankles, and his waist had all been tied down to the bed with strong fabric straps. He knew he was no longer in his hotel room. Someone had carried him out of his room. Lying there struggling to get himself free, he recounted last night. "The wine," he thought to himself. "Someone drugged the wine."

As Bishop lay in the strange bed, he tried to look around the room to figure out where he was. The room was old and bare. It looked like it had been abandoned decades earlier. The bed was a simple metal frame with a mattress. The straps securing Bishop were tied to the rusty metal frame. Bishop began shaking the bed and yanking on the straps, trying to break free. The harder he shook the bed, the higher the bed began lifting off the ground. He grabbed onto the bed frame to generate more force. With each pull and lift, the bed frame loosened more and more. He could now see the frame beginning to separate. "Come on!," he said. "Come on!" One more strong yank and the bed frame snapped and his right arm became free. He untied himself and snapped off a section of the bed frame to use a as a weapon. The room he was in had no door, so he walked into a hallway. Immediately he realized that he was in an abandoned house. Quietly, he walked along the wall of the hallway. He came to what was once a living room, and saw that the house was empty. "What the hell is going on?" he thought to himself. He heard a sound coming from another room. He backed up against the wall and walked toward the kitchen. He could hear voices in the kitchen talking. It sounded like an Eastern European dialect.

Bishop sprang into the room and grabbed one of the men who was sitting down at the table. Bishop pressed the metal pole into the man's neck enough to draw blood and yelled at the other two men to put their hands behind their heads. "Do it! Now!" he demanded. The men did as he instructed and Bishop started demanding answers. "Who are you? Where am I? Who hired you?" The men just sat there and stared back at Bishop, so he pushed the small pole a little deeper into the man's neck. The man began screaming and yelling in his native language. "English! English!" Bishop said.

"We don't know his name," one of them said. "A carrier brings money in the mail. I've never met him. I have only spoken to him one time on the phone."

"Carrier?" Bishop asked. "You mean courier?"

"Yes," the man said nervously.

Bishop knew that this was the same "mystery man." This had to be Jefferson Clark. Bishop pulled the small hand gun out of his captive's belt and pointed it at his head. "Everyone stay right there," Bishop said, as he stepped backward. He used the man he was holding as a shield and slowly backed out of the room. The other three sat there, waiting for the moment Bishop went out of sight, so that they could grab their guns and go after him. He backed out of the room and the three men heard a loud thud. They got up and ran into the other room to find the man Bishop used as makeshift shield unconscious on the floor. They ran to the front door and did not see Bishop. They split up and began searching for him.

Right when they left the house, Bishop dropped down from the ceiling where he was hiding on top of a large wooden beam that was exposed above them. He quickly searched the house for any clue of who may have hired these guys. He searched for the better part of five minutes and didn't find a single bit of evidence that told him who hired the abductors. He looked at his watch and saw that he needed to get out of there because his captors could be back any second, so he found the door to the backyard and quickly left.

Bishop arrived back at his hotel and found the security room. He wanted to look at the video surveillance footage of last night. Maybe he could find out more about who hired the abductors. He knocked on the door to see if anyone was there. "Hello? Can you open the door please?" Bishop knocked a second time, no answer. The door was locked and only opened with a magnetic strip card, similar to that of a regular hotel room. He looked around and saw the concierge, an attractive young woman whom under other circumstances Bishop might try asking out for a drink. He approached her desk and along the way he grabbed a tourist map of Rome. "Excuse me, miss?" he said politely.

He stopped at a small table across from the concierge desk, intentionally drawing her to him. "I'm having trouble finding the Trevi Fountain." An obvious rouse by Bishop, it's hard to miss an eighty-five foot tall fountain, but because Bishop was so charming, the young woman was much obliged to help the lost tourist. She leaned over Bishop to point out where the fountain was and where they were in relation to it on the map. As the two shared an intimately close space, Bishop looked directly into her light emerald eyes as if to say, "How about we go find an unoccupied room?" In their moment of flirting, Bishop reached down and removed the security key from her belt. He leaned in even closer to her ear and whispered, "Sei un angelo." In any language, telling a woman she's "an angel" is a pretty sure fire way to warm a heart.

After stealing the security key, Bishop left the young concierge. He gave her a smile and made it back to the security room and opened the door. Inside he found a network of security screens monitoring all of the hotel. He looked around and found a cabinet with date-labeled DVDs. He saw one labeled "elevators," with the date and time that corresponded with the time he was in his room. He put the disk into one of the players and fast forwarded through it until he came to 9:52 pm which was when was checking in at the front desk. On the screen he saw a man resembling one of his abductors, wearing a room service uniform and carrying the bottle of wine that was left in his room. Two hours further along on the tape, Bishop identified the same man, along with two other men that he also recognized as the men from the house, enter an elevator . . . still no sign of who hired them.

Bishop then thought to check where they exited. He forwarded to the point where he saw the men walking, dragging him into the elevator. He could plainly see himself in the tape so he proceeded to look for the footage of the men leaving the building. Bishop knew that the hotel had a rear entrance that was not visible to anyone from within the hotel, but he knew there was a camera pointed at the door. He went back to the cabinet and located the correct camera footage. After viewing the video, Bishop once again came up empty. He could not see anyone on the tape, other than the men carrying him out. He was now even more determined to find out who was trying to stop him from investigating. He left the hotel and went to the Banca d'Italia.

Bishop arrived at the Bank and asked the manager what types of financial holdings they offered? The manager informed him that they primarily dealt with Vatican City holdings. Bishop was perplexed and intrigued because he knew that Vatican City had a Banking system of its own; why would a Bank of Italy be in control of Vatican finances? The further he inquired about the bank's business, the fewer answers he received. This was quickly becoming a dead end, but he now knew that whomever had an account here, must have some connection to someone within the Vatican. "Um, just one quick last question and I'll be on my way . . . Who is the President of the bank?"

At this point, the manager just wanted to get rid of Bishop and answered him in a very annoyed tone. "The Chairman is Signore William Carter. Now if you don't mind, I am very busy today."

"William Carter?" Bishop couldn't believe it. The chairman of the bank is related to Jefferson Carter. Bishop's head was swirling with thoughts of conspiracy. He quickly got on the phone with Donald, "I'm on my way to the airport, I'll be back in London in a couple of hours. What I just found out will blow your mind," he said.

When Bishop arrived back in London, he was met at the airport by Donald on the tarmac. The two got into Donald's car and drove toward Manchester so they could get Bishop back for his concert. "So what did you find out in Rome,?" Donald asked.

"Well, first off, someone does not want me looking into any of this. I was drugged and kidnapped last night from my hotel room," Bishop said half amused.

"What?" Donald was mildly shocked by how calm Bishop was while recalling his near deathly experience.

"But that was really all in a day's work, I suppose. The interesting part is what I found out at the bank. It turns out that the chairman of the Banca d'Italia is none other than William Carter. What do you suppose the chances are that William Carter is related to Jefferson Carter?" Bishop said.

"I would say almost certainly," Donald replied. "I'll get on the phone with the State Department and find out everything I can about the Banca d'Italia and William Carter. I'd say it's about time you found out more about Jefferson Carter."

They drove all the way back to Manchester where Bishop met up with his band. When he got to the hotel, Bishop found James in the bar having a drink. "What's up man!" Bishop said excitedly.

"Hey, dick . . . where were you last night?" James questioned. The rest of the band got to Manchester the night before. The morning after their show in Berlin, the band flew from Berlin to

Manchester. When they got there, Bishop went to see his contact Jenkins, while the rest of the band went to the hotel.

"Oh yeah, I just wasn't feeling that great. I stayed in my room and slept pretty much the whole time. I'm feeling much better now though," Bishop replied.

"Another beer for my friend," James said to the bartender.

"Thanks, man."

The two were chatting for a few minutes when three beautiful women came in and sat at the bar. Bishop and James gave each other a quick look and a smile, as if to say, "Oh yeah, they're hot." The women, three Americans on vacation in Europe, were celebrating their recent college graduation. "Americans?" James asked.

"Oh my god! You too?" One of them exclaimed with exuberance.

"I'm James . . ." he said, "and this is Bishop."

"I'm Kara, hi . . . and this is Stefanie and Trisha," she said.

"Hi," they all said in unison.

"JINX!" Kara said. "Now you owe me a shot."

"A shot? What the hell happened to owing you a Coke?" Bishop asked playfully.

"That was when we were kids," she said.

"Oh, you're a big girl now? You get a big girl drink instead?"

"Exactly," she laughed. She smiled and batted her almond shape, light brown eyes.

"Bartender," Bishop called out. "A round of whiskey here for my friends." They all gave out exclamations in excitement. "So where are you ladies from?"

"We just graduated from Warner."

"Ah . . . the 'Harvard of the Midwest' right?"

Kara smiled and said, "Oh, you know it? Where are you guys from?"

"New York, originally, its been so long since I've been home though, I'm surprised I know that."

"Mmmm, now that sounds like there's a story there." She leaned in and squeezed his thigh in an overtly flirtatious manner.

"Well, after I graduated high school I joined the Army. I went to Bosnia. Then, after I was discharged, I came back home and met up with this guy and we started a band. We've been touring non-stop, pretty much since we got started. That's why we're here in England, Europe actually."

"You're touring Europe? What's your band? You guys must be pretty good," she said.

"I'm the singer of *Fighter,* and James here plays guitar."

"Shut . . . Up." Kara's response was that of shock and awe.

"Oh, you know us?" Bishop said in a similar voice as Kara, attempting to be coy.

The bartender placed the shots of the house brand whiskey, which was actually a pretty good selection, in front of the patrons.

"Oh my god!" Kara said and turned to her friends. "These guys are in *Fighter.* Can you believe that?"

The girls' faces lit up. Bishop passed the shots out and held his glass up to make a toast. "Here's to good friends, good times, happy thoughts, happy lives, as long or as short as they me be . . . Salud!"

They sat and drank for an hour, laughing, talking, doing everything Bishop needed to do to decompress from his reconnaissance in Rome. Before they left, Bishop and James gave the girls passes to the show that night and told them to meet them backstage after the show.

When they got to the theater, they arrived to a sea of people waiting in front of the entrance. The SUVs pulled up to the side of the theater and the guys got out and ran inside the back entrance. They couldn't hold back their smiles and laughter as they were ushered into the building; they felt like the Beatles.

Once again they played to an adoring full crowd that sang along to almost every song that Fighter played. As Bishop stood front and center of the stage behind his microphone, he suddenly was struck by emotion. The realization of how unique his life was, the pure joy he gave to his fans, the patriotic work he did for his country, and the memory of his parents and how they never got a chance to see him succeed, all hit him at once. Fortunately for Bishop, when he was taken back by that sudden surge of emotion, James was performing a solo because Bishop found himself a little bit lost in the moment.

He gathered himself and started singing.

"Chasing a dream,

But this dream runs too fast,
Running hard, till I just can't run anymore,
You're the only one to catch me when I stumble and fall . . ."

The show ended and they returned backstage and briefly celebrated another great show. Kara and her friends from the bar walked into the small room just as Bishop and the guys finished congratulating each other on another great show. The night that ensued was filled with debaucheries that would make other notorious rock stars look like choir boys. The morning after, which seemed like a millennium later, the girls left Fighter's hotel, never to be heard from again . . . the perfect relationship for a rock star.

Fighter finished their European tour, playing twelve more shows across western Europe, none as memorable as that night in Manchester. When they were done, the four flew back home to New York for some much needed rest and relaxation before beginning a small American tour the following month. Bishop went to his new home in Connecticut, just long enough to pack a few things for his trip to Louisiana. What he had discovered about Jefferson Carter could not wait any longer. He needed to start investigating him immediately.

Chapter 8

Hi, I'm Jason Trudeaux

Most people would tell you that Jefferson Carter was a nice southern gentleman. However, most people did not truly know him. The man most people knew was a philanthropist of sorts, a wealthy entrepreneur and business man who gave generously to the community. He was a fifth generation southerner from the state of Louisiana. The Carter family was made from a long line of oil men. The lineage went back to Jefferson's great-grandfather, William Carter, who discovered a natural gas deposit in northern Louisiana while drilling a well. From that point on, the Carter family searched for and found natural gas and oil all over Louisiana and built up one of the largest oil producing companies in the United States.

Besides being quite charismatic, Carter was also very intelligent and physically strong. An avid golfer and fitness junkie, Carter spent his weekend mornings on the golf course and ritualistically ran five miles every morning. He was in his mid forties and he had the fitness level of an in-shape thirty year old. Standing at an imposing six foot four, he had a stature that intimidated his competitors and impressed his admirers. He had a partiality for wearing vests. He owned just about every color and style one could imagine, one for every outfit he owned . . . and they were all classy and sophisticated. His deep blue eyes were always a conversation piece for the many admiring women he met, and he had a small scar on his jaw that gave Jefferson Carter's face an element of ruggedness that offset any snobbish high-class society his persona gave.

Even though his scar gave a "working man's" appearance to Carter, his true nature and personality was that of extreme ego and entitlement. He grew up wealthy and he always felt better than anyone else because of it. As he got older and started taking over the family business, he became less and less satisfied with the size of the corporation. He wanted more. The size of the man's ego and his own perception of his "role" in Louisiana could be summed up by taking a look at the name plate on his personal desk which read, "Jefferson Carter: CEO of Louisiana." He craved success so desperately, that at times his ego clouded his ability to make smart decisions.

Always being the entrepreneur, Carter was constantly looking for the next big business venture. He had three oil production plants in Louisiana and one in Saudi Arabia that his father silently purchased in the early 1970's . . . before the Saudi government seized full control of the, at the time, American Arabian Oil Company. Some of his other business ventures included commercial real estate, a small agricultural investment in honey production, and a failed attempt at producing music.

Jefferson Carter had what you call, "old money." The majority of his wealth was established by his father and grandfather, and then passed on to him. It was likely because of this that Carter was really quite flawed in some respects. He didn't have a real sense of reality, right or wrong, and he was very sheltered and spoiled. Carter's' entire goal in life was to be more monetarily successful than his grandfather and father. Since both had passed away, along with his mother two years after his father, Carter's only form of parental approval and recognition of success was what he imagined in his head. It was that lack of validation that led to Carter's endless pursuit of financial success, and at times the line of ethical business practices were blurred and sometimes blatantly thrown by the way side.

Carter wanted to separate himself from the rest of the energy producing world, and he was determined to do that with nuclear hybrid technology. As a way of obtaining the raw nuclear materials for his new hybrid technology, Carter went to a black market arms dealer and bought enough uranium to create a nuclear powered, thermo chemical energy source the world had never seen. If successful, this new form of energy production had the potential to supply energy to millions of homes and businesses at a minimal cost. The technology also could be sustainable in automobiles, rendering petroleum based automobiles a thing of the past. This new thermo chemical energy source could easily be transported in a liquid hydrogen form, to a nuclear generated power plant and then sustain the power plant on thermo chemical technology.

Bishop arrived at the Naval Air Station just south of the city of New Orleans. He arranged for a car to be waiting for him near the airfield. He grabbed his two carry-on bags and exited the plane. It was a gorgeous mid- morning in early October. The warm sun beamed down onto Bishop's face as he stepped down the steps of the airplane. He paused for a moment as he reached the bottom and allowed the calm relaxing warmth of the sun to bask on his face. He got into his car and entered the address of Jefferson Carter's oil field into the car's gps. He began driving toward Baton Rouge, where Carter's largest mainland oil field was located. He was driving northwest through New Orleans when memories of his time in the Army there began to surface. He thought to himself "One day, I'm gonna actually enjoy seeing this city."

He finally arrived at Carter Petroleum and Energy in Baton Rouge. He had with him, a fake I.D. badge from Tulane University. Bishop was posing as a graduate student, researching alternative energy for his fake Masters Degree. The day before he left for New Orleans, he called Carter Petroleum and scheduled a tour of the facility, not knowing if Carter would actually be there or not, but he decided to take his chances anyway.

The building seen from the street was a typical industrial office building. It was three stories tall and extended out for about a hundred yards. The paint on the exterior was a bland pale yellow color. Everything from the outside screamed inconspicuous. Bishop pulled to the front, which was guarded by a toll booth guard. Bishop said to the man, "Hi, I'm Jason Trudeaux, from Tulane. I'm here for a tour."

The man looked down at a clipboard to check for scheduled appointments. Bishop sat in his luxury rental car that he had arranged to be at the airport. As he sat there, Bishop began to get nervous because the guard was taking what seemed to be a very long time to find his name on the appointment list. "Here you are Mr. Trudeaux," the guard said. He handed Bishop a temporary parking pass to hang from his rearview mirror. "Just follow this road here, and make a left at the stop sign. The main building will be on your right. Go right in and speak with the receptionist. She'll instruct you where to go."

"Thank you sir," Bishop said. He drove in and followed the street to the main building. As he slowly drove through the complex, he tried to take in everything he could see from his car. He noticed three buildings in the complex, and a fourth building farther up a hill that had its own gate and security guarding it.

He parked his car and hung his navy blue temporary parking pass on his mirror. He chuckled when he saw the pass hanging from the mirror. It was the same color of his high school parking pass that he also hung from his mirror a decade before. The same one that one day, he and James had the "hilarious" idea to take their school parking passes and swipe them up the butt cracks of their schoolmates, saying "Credit Card!" as they walked by in the halls. The kids jumped and everyone laughed hysterically. It was a fond memory for Bishop, especially under the circumstances.

Bishop got out of his car and walked up to the building and entered through the heavily tinted glass doors. The secretary, an attractive bruenette was on the phone. "Mr. Robins is out of the office today, may I take a message?" she said. Bishop walked over and casually sat on the corner of her desk and smiled. "I'll let him know sir, good-bye," she replied to a caller and hung up the phone but in the same breath she looked at Bishop and said, "Can I help you with something while you get off my desk?"

Bishop scooted off the desk and introduced himself, "Hi, Jason Trudeaux. I'm here for a tour."

She lowered her head to look down at her appointments and as she lowered her head, she kept her eyes fixated on Bishop. His magnetic, flirtatious personality had reeled her in. When she had lowered her head down enough, she read out loud, "From Tulane? Mr. Scott will be showing you around. Go ahead and have a seat over there and I'll let Mr. Scott know you are here."

Bishop sat down in a cold tan leather chair that was across from the receptionist. "No one sits here very often, do they?" Bishop asked. "These chairs have got to be the most uncomfortable chairs ever." He was attempting to be playful and flirtatious with the secretary, who appeared to no longer be entertained at all by Bishop's behavior. "I didn't catch your name," he said. She just continued typing on her computer, trying her best to ignore him.

"Jason? Jason Trudeaux?" a voice said from behind him. Bishop stood up and turned around. "Hi there, I'm Larry Scott. I understand you're doing your Master's Thesis on alternative energy." Larry Scott was a portly, balding middle-aged man with an infectious personality. Everyone around Carter Petroleum loved Larry Scott. He was the guy that when you didn't have much to do, and you just wanted to talk to someone, Larry was that guy you'd go to. Larry could talk for hours to anyone about anything, and he had the courtesy and good sense to stop talking when you've heard enough. "What do you say we head over to our media room, and I'll give you a run down on what we do here? Then we'll head over to the 'fields." Carter Petroleum in Baton Rouge was built on acres upon acres of swamp land that was now home to fields upon fields of oil derricks.

The presentation took well over an hour. As entertaining as Larry Scott was, making Bishop interested in the petroleum processes was a near impossibility. On two occassions, Bishop had to prevent himself from falling asleep. He was convinced that he did not need to see anymore of this. What he did need to know was what Jefferson Carter had to do with O'Connor and his relationship to William Carter in Rome.

"Mr. Scott, I thank you for your time. I learned a lot here today. Unfortunately, I need to get back. I have another appointment this afternoon. I really appreciate your time," Bishop said. He stood up and shook Larry's hand. "I know you're a busy man, I remember the way out. I can find it."

The two shook hands and Bishop started going towards the main entrance until Larry Scott was out of sight. Bishop had to find Carter's office. "He must have an office here some place, Bishop thought. He could either go snooping around for hours, trying to find Carter's office, or he could just go ask somebody who could just tell him where it was.

Bishop approached the secretary's desk smiling. "So . . . do I get to know your name?" he asked.

She looked at him expressionless and then cracked a smile. "Cindy, how are you?" she said.

"Cindy, I'm doing pretty well today, but you know what would make this an exceptional day? If you could tell me where I can find Jefferson Carter's office, I would be so grateful.

He smiled at her, using his ever charming look. It was only a matter of time before she cracked.

"It's on the third floor. Once you exit the elevator, it's all the way down the right hallway," she said.

"Cindy, you are a savior . . . no, wait . . . you are MY savior," he said. The corniness was so over the top that she couldn't help but laugh. Bishop was just far too charming to resist a laugh.

Bishop went to the elevator and got off on the third floor, like Cindy instructed him. He walked down the hallway, passing a long window that rose from the floor all the way to the ceiling, and stretched the length of the hallway. As he got closer, he could hear a secretary speaking to someone. "Mr. Carter will be available tomorrow after 3:00 pm." She was obviously speaking to someone on the phone, "Yes, that is correct. You have a nice day too," she said. Bishop walked up and introduced himself.

"Hello, my name is Jason Trudeaux. I'm with the U.S. Enviromental Protection Agency. I am going to need a few minutes to speak with Mr. Carter and I am on a tight schedule. Is he in?"

Bishop was becoming very comfortable with playing different characters. He was now even becoming so comfortable as to use accents, like the southern accent he was now using with Jefferson Carter's secretary. "Yes he is, just one moment please," she said.

She picked up a phone and pressed one of the buttons. He must have picked up quickly because almost immediately after pressing the button she said, "Sir, there is a Jason Trudeaux from the EPA here to see you." There was a momentary pause, then she said, "Mr. Carter will see you right now."

A large cherry wood desk guarded Jefferson Carter. Two large high definition flat screen televisions hung side by side on a wall.

The room was a stark contrast to the rest of the building. Carter's office had a sophistication and high class décor, while the rest of the building was very average looking. "Mr. Trudeaux, how can I help the EPA today?" Carter said.

Bishop's suspicions and hunches of Carter being dirty, were all the more solidified by the appearance of Carter's office. For everything that Bishop knew and suspected about Carter, it took some restraint from Bishop not to just hand Carter over to the State Department. However, he realized that most, if not everything he had on Carter, could be circumstantial. After all, it's not against the law to have a fine taste for interior decorating. Carter's elaborately-expensive ornate furnishings could have been paid for with his oil money, but something about the whole situation seemed a bit "off" to Bishop. It just felt like he walked into a "Bond" villain's lair.

"I'm doing well Mr. Carter," Bishop replied. "You have quite the operation going on here. How much does an operation like this bring in, in a year?" Bishop was clearly trying to antagonize Jefferson Carter by choosing his words carefully, calling his company an operation as if to insinuate a more nefarious situation was at hand.

"Mr. Trudeaux, I assure you that everything that we do here is for the betterment of society," Carter said.

"Does the betterment of society involve uranium, Mr. Carter?" Bishop went straight to the point. "Call me crazy, but I'm the kind of guy who believes that private citizens building nuclear weapons is not for the betterment of society."

Carter responded abruptly, "Okay, you got me Mr. Trudeaux. The truth is, I'm a capitalist. Greed and the pursuit of personal happiness are what rules us. The idea of a moral and ethical society is an imaginative farce . . . and furthermore, I would watch what you say to me, Mr. Trudeaux. I am not someone to be taken lightly." Carter began to stall with Bihop while he searched the EPA database on his computer for the personnel file on Jason Trudeaux. As expected, Carter's sources through his illegal computer network found no record of Jason Trudeaux in the EPA.

"How about you tell me about William Carter? What is your relation to him?" he asked.

"Do you like chess Mr. Trudeaux?" Carter asked as he stood up from his desk. "There's a point in every game where you are feeling each other out, trying to figure out your opponent's strategy . . . and all the while one person is planning an attack. They're planning for the kill, while the other person is still trying to figure out the other's strategy. Do you know which player you are Mr. Trudeaux? Are you still trying to figure me out?"

Just then, four burly security guards entered the room. Carter had pressed the big red security alarm button underneath his desk. The four guards measured in at an average of six foot five, three-hundred and ten pounds. The four men resembled an All-Pro offensive line, in fact two of them did play professionally briefly in Canada before being banned for repeatedly violating the league's steroid policy, and one tested positive for Finaplix, a horse anabolic steroid.

"This conversation is over. Please escort Mr. Trudeaux out of the building," Carter said. "I am many things, Mr. Trudeaux, but a murderer I am not, but I will go to whatever lengths necessary to protect my investments. But let me give you some advice: What you are pursuing is not what you think it is, nor am I the one you are really after."

"So I suppose you're gonna tell me you didn't have people in England and in Rome try to kill me?" Bishop responded.

"As I just said, I am not a murderer. Whoever is trying to kill you, I'm sure they will resolve their issue with you shortly, but I am not that person. In fact Mr. Trudeaux, if I really wanted to kill you, you and I would not be having this conversation," Carter said. "Now . . . my agenda should be of no concern to you, Mr. Trudeaux, so if you know what's best for you, you will go about your business and leave Carter Petroleum alone. I know people who can make other people's lives miserable."

The guards walked Bishop from the office to an elevator just outside of Carter's office. The five men snuggly fit into the elevator, two in front of Bishop and two behind. Bishop turned his head and looked at Xavier, the head of Carter's security and the one smaller, semi-normal looking guy and said, "Do we know each other?" A familiarity struck Bishop when he looked at Xavier, but he couldn't place from where. The man just continued looking forward.

"So where do you guys shop for suits?" It was obvious by the look of these guys that buying suits off of the rack was not an option.

Bishop turned his head and looked at one of the other henchmen and said, "You know I ask because a guy I know, he's a big guy too . . . well not quite like you. You're like something out of Greek mythology . . . but anyway this guy I know, he has trouble shopping for suits as well." The four guards just stood there silently as the elevator descended to the ground level. "Tough room," Bishop said to himself.

Bishop was all the more confused, for some bizarre reason he felt like Carter was telling the truth. There was something else that Bishop was missing. Carter was not the "big fish" that Bishop should be pursuing.

Someone else ordered the men in Europe to go after him, Bishop surmised. He was convinced that Carter was not developing a weapon, but something for his own personal gain. It was clear to Bishop that the mystery man who shot O'Conner was not Jefferson Carter. Bishop had to find the man who sold the uranium to Carter. This was the man who he should've been pursuing from the start. Bishop realized that Carter himself was afraid of the man who sold him the uranium.

He started driving back to New Orleans and couldn't shake the thought of finding the mystery man . . . BANG! The loud bang startled Bishop. He started losing control of his car so he pulled over to the side of the road to check his tires. He was five miles from any kind of city, and the population of gators and water-moccasins outnumbered the number of people residing in the area.

He got out and walked to the rear of the car. The rear driver's side tire was blown out and shredded down to the rim. He popped the trunk to search for a spare. Just as he was opening his trunk, a large tow truck was pulling up. The driver rolled down his window and Bishop said, "Wow, talk about timing. I just had a blow-out."

The driver looked down at Bishop and said, "Mr. Trudeaux?" Bishop immediately knew something was up. This is not a tow truck driver. How did he know who he was? Bishop started to reach under his jacket for his Glock 19 when the driver lifted up his gun and shot Bishop in the chest. The driver of the truck calmly hopped out and picked Bishop up off the ground and placed him in the truck.

The driver, an average height, athletically built man who was very neatly groomed and clean-shaven, did not resemble the average tow truck driver. This man was more like central casting for a day-time soap opera. He drove Bishop to a shack in the woods that hunters use during gator season. Along the way, Bishop woke up but he could not move. The driver had shot him with a tranquilizer gun, leaving him in a temporary paralyzed state. Bishop was able to just barely move his right hand enough to press a small button on his wrist watch that activated a distress signal.

They arrived at the shack where the driver was met by two other men dressed in suits, which was not exactly the appropriate attire for walking around in the Bayou. They took Bishop inside and as they entered the building, Bishop suddenly had enough strength to try and make an escape. He shoved the truck driver to the ground and kicked the man in front of him. Bishop turned and grabbed the door handle, but the other men were too alert and fast for Bishop. They grabbed him and threw him against a table in the middle of the room. He tried to bounce back up, but as he struggled to get to his feet, he heard the iconic sound of a gun being cocked, followed by a voice.

"Sit down." Bishop sat down in one of the chairs and one of the men pulled out a pair of handcuffs. Bishop jumped out of the chair only to be grabbed and overpowered by two of the men. They forced him back down into the chair, and the man with the handcuffs bound Bishop's arms behind his back so that he could not stand up from the chair.

"You have quite the fight in you, Mr. Trudeaux," the man said. The man was Xavier, a notorious gun for hire. He had worked for numerous organized crime bosses in the United States and in Europe. It was rumored that Xavier had killed in excess of seventy individuals. If you were involved in organized crime in any way, trying to stop it or trying to profit from it, and you had an unexpected visit from Xavier, that meant your time on Earth was up. He was so notorious in crime circles that he earned the nickname, The Reaper.

The men left the room and then minutes later Xavier re-entered the room. He stepped in front of Bishop, facing him so that Bishop could see the soldering iron he was holding. "I am going to ask that you tell me who you are," Xavier said. "I know that you are going to lie to me, and I know that we will have to go back and forth with the questions and answers because you won't really know just how serious this will get . . . so I will go ahead and show you what will happen to you if you do not tell me what I want to know. You understand that this is for your own sake. I am going to remove one of your toes, using this soldering iron. I imagine it will be quite painful, so do yourself a favor and be honest with me when I am done. Okay? All right, lets get started shall we?"

Xavier cut away Bishop's laces and removed one of his shoes and socks. Bishop began breathing heavily and his heart started to race. Xavier lit the ominous soldering iron and slowly lowered it to Bishop's left foot. The smell of burning flesh filled the room as Xavier began burning off Bishop's left big toe. He screamed and spat in Xavier's face. After about fifteen seconds, the pain had actually subsided while adrenaline and shock took over.

When he had finished, Xavier looked up at Bishop and said, "Okay, now that that's out of the way, why don't you tell me your name and who you work for."

Bishop was on the verge of passing out. He didn't know how far away Donald was, and he could not last much longer. He needed to say something that would buy him some time. "My name is Trudeaux," he said.

After a pause, Xavier punched Bishop and said, "And who do you work for?" These torturous interrogations were beginning to become a nuisance, to say the least, for Bishop. Losing a toe was not exactly what he had envisioned when he decided to interview Jefferson Carter.

"Continental Energy," Bishop responded. The first thing that came to mind was Carter Petroleum's biggest competitor. "I work for Continental Energy." This was only going to buy Bishop a short amount of time before they figured out that Bishop did not work for Continenetal Energy. Xavier left the room and came back five minutes later. Bishop was fading in and out of consciousness.

A man walked into the room and stood in front of Bishop. He was a debonair looking man, a shoe-in for the cover of GQ Magazine. He had light brown eyes with a complection that was once naturally more pale, but is now tan. He had dark hair with gray in his sideburns that led up the sides just above his ears. He was dressed in a black suit and the cornflower blue breast pocket hankerchief was an exact match to his shirt. "Mr. Trudeaux," the man said. "I do not appreciate people interfering with my business."

The man was even colder than Xavier. He showed no emotion toward Bishop. "Who are you?" Bishop asked.

"The fact that I have kept my identity unknown to anyone I don't want to know, has been very profitable to me," the man said. "You have been spending a lot of time and energy investigating my business, Mr. Trudeaux. It's a shame that your investigation will end so soon. Goodbye Mr. Trudeaux." Xavier and the mystery man left the room and Bishop could hear the sound of a car drive away. The remaining men went outside and brought in a large plastic tarp and a chainsaw. Bishop knew he was gator bait.

His heart began racing as the man started the saw. The sound of a chainsaw always carries a hint of potential danger to it, but when you're faced with someone who's intending to use it on you, "hint of danger" doesn't quite live up to the actual emotion it evokes.

His forehead was dripping with sweat and his body was beginning to tense up, but before the men could start their "work", the door to the shack flew open. Ten CIA agents burst into the room and shot the remaining henchmen cold in their tracks. "Taking your time Donald?" Bishop said as Paul Donald walked into the room. Bishop gave an auditory sigh of relief.

CHAPTER 9

LOVE NEVER FADES

Bishop was about to resume the tour with Fighter. They had a three week break between the conclusion of their European tour and the start of their North American tour. Bishop spent the entire three week break, recuperating from losing his toe. His thoughts were still consumed with what had happened. He could occasionally close his eyes and still see Xavier. His face was emblazoned into Bishop's mind. Because the band was taking a vacation between tours, the other guys in Fighter had not seen Bishop since his ordeal. This gave Bishop time to conceal his wounds and try to get used to walking with only nine toes.

For about a week, Bishop went to physical therapy. At first, it was tedious and painful, but each subsequent day was easier than the next due to "smoking hot" brunette therapist who was there. He never did muster the courage to ask her out, instead he just stared and smiled at her like mental patient.

The band met each other in New York to rehearse new material which was also the location of their first show of their North American tour. They were going to start it off in New York and then five shows around the New England area, before going up to Canada and then back through the Midwest and on to California. On the second day at the recording studio in New York, Bishop introduced a few songs he had written. He strummed gently on his guitar as he sang some of his lyrics. *"I call it, Me, Me, Me,"* he said.

"I fell in love
But that's not what you said
I thought I was with you
But you were alone
I had a dream that we would be we
All you ever thought about was me, me, me
All you ever thought about was me, me, me

Memories and laughing reminders
Of you are burning up in my mind
False embraces and insincere faces
Are all I have left of you
I had a dream that we would be we
All you ever thought about was me, me, me
All you ever thought about was me, me, me"

"Let me guess, you've been listening to The Cure a lot haven't you?" James said. The room chuckled. "No, in all seriousness, it's good. I think I have a melody for that." James picked up his guitar and started playing a tune. "Start it from the top again." They began to put the song together, playing with the melody and changing some of the lyrics to a point that they were satisfied with it and began to record. They played for the better part of 13 hours that day at the recording studio and at James' apartment in the city. They recorded three songs and they were gleaming with anticipation of completing the album. They rehearsed and recorded for the rest of the week, preparing themselves for their first show in New York.

The first show on the North American tour was a bit of a struggle for Fighter. Bishop's foot suddenly became an issue half way through the show when he started experiencing a sharp pain that was shooting all the way up to his knee. He managed to play through the pain, but Bishop's injury wasn't the only problem with the show. Between the second and third song, James changed guitars and when he began strumming to the next song he realized that the guitar was not tuned properly. After a brief moment, he got his guitar back in tune and they played on. After the few setbacks, Fighter lived up to their name and fought through whatever adversity had presented itself. The next couple of shows went much smoother and Bishop's foot was becoming less and less of an issue.

The set lists for each show were getting longer and they were now playing two hour shows as opposed to an hour, to an hour and a half. They were now playing the new songs in their shows Fighter had been rehearsing for an upcoming album.

At their Boston show, they were finishing one of their last songs when Bishop looked out into the crowd and he thought he saw a familiar face. It was for a split second but long enough for him to think to himself, "Was that . . .?" They started playing their final song, "The Blame" when he found the face in the crowd again. He was certain it was her. The first glance he thought maybe he was imagining it or maybe he just saw someone who resembled her, but it was her. It was Mary Wilson.

After the show ended, all Bishop could think about was Mary. He had to find her. He was back stage in his dressing room when he received a letter from one of the security guards at the theater. The letter read, "Connie's Diner, 12:30 am - a friend." He knew it was her. His heart raced, thinking about her. He was a little bit older now, and finding someone he cared for was something he couldn't pass up. All of the horrifying things he had to endure for his "job," it was all beginning to get old and pointless for him. There seemed to be no gratifying light at the end of the proverbial tunnel for him if he continued working for Donald.

His palms were sweaty. He looked at his watch, 12:22 a.m. it read. He was standing in front of the diner and his stomach was fluttering and churning like never before. He had faced certain death and grave situations numerous times, but the idea of reuniting with Mary made him more nervous than death-defying challenge he had ever faced in his young life. Bishop walked inside and sat down in a booth near the window and waited. The minutes went by agonizingly slow. Each time he glanced down at his watch he thought that it had stopped because of how slowly the minutes passed. It was now 12:31 and no sign of Mary. It was only a minute past, and Bishop started thinking that she wouldn't show. "Finally", at 12:33 the door opened and Mary walked in the door.

She looked just like he remembered her, still the most beautiful girl in the room without any level of arrogance about her. She knew she was attractive and owned her sex appeal, but her kindness and compassion, her down-to-earth nature gave her another level of attractiveness and likeability. She was wearing dark blue jeans with red high heels with a black leather jacket over her Iron Maiden, Killers t-shirt that gave her a little bit of edginess.

Bishop stood up as she approached his booth and opened his arms to give her a hug. She wrapped her arms around him in an embrace that was both friendly and kind, as well as loving and passionate. While still holding on to him, she said, "It's so good to see you again. It's been too long." They sat down across from each other in a booth, each smiling as they both absorbed the moment. From outside of the diner, to anyone passing by, it looked like a photograph or a famous painting. A man and a woman smiling and laughing in the window of an empty diner late at night.

"I can't believe you came like this . . ." he said, "this is awesome."

"I thought I saw you limping a little bit. Are you okay? What happened?" she asked.

Bishop was so caught up in the moment of being with her again, that the truth almost came out of his mouth. "Oh that, it . . . uh . . . yeah, I was . . . and this thing . . . on my foot . . . bang! Um, it was an accident. I dropped a big speaker on my toe a few weeks ago and I actually needed to have it amputated."

Mary was shocked in horror and concern. "Oh my God. Are you serious? That's terrible, I'm so sorry. Do you need any other surgeries? Are you going to be okay?"

"No . . . Yeah, yeah. I'm fine. I'll be fine. No, I don't need more surgery. I'm still getting used to it, but doctors have told me that I should be just fine after I adjust to nine toes," he chuckled.

She was being concerned for her friend, but she couldn't help the humor from building up inside of her. "So, do you get a discount when you shop for shoes?" The two sat in silence for a few seconds before they both started laughing uncontrollably. "I'm sorry," she said as she laughed even harder which made Bishop start to laugh even harder.

"I guess I have to accept the fact that I'll never be a ballet dancer now," he said jokingly. They laughed the entire night. They caught up on their lives, exchanging stories of what they each had been through since they last saw each other. Mary told Bishop about her new career as a columnist for the Baltimore Herald and how she did finally finish her novel, but never had the courage to try and get it published. Her fear of rejection was all too great. She was content with the personal achievement of just actually writing a novel.

Just like when they were teenagers at the ice cream shop, Bishop and Mary sat at the diner talking for hours only this time they talked until the sun came up. By 6:20 a.m., they both were getting exhausted. Bishop said to Mary, "Would you like to come back to my hotel . . . to sleep, that is?"

Mary thought about it for a second, or at least gave the impression that she was thinking about and said, "Yes." The two got a cab and drove to the hotel in Boston where Fighter was staying. The band wasn't scheduled to leave for Toronto until the next day, so Bishop and Mary could have the entire day to spend together.

When they got back to the hotel, they were still acting like teenagers. They laughed and giggled as they walked through the hotel lobby, making the hotel manager raise his eyebrows in disapproval. They were standing at the elevators waiting for the doors to open, but spontaneity took over and Mary grabbed Bishop's hand and led him to the stairwell instead.

They started walking up the stairs and made it to the second story when Mary turned around and faced Bishop from the top of the stairs. Her expression quickly went from laughing to seduction as she looked into his eyes. It was more than enough for Bishop to passionately hold the back of her head and pull her in closer. The kiss between them was so romantic, so passionate, so incredible that if a 10.0 mega-earthquake hit at that moment and the walls came crumbling down around them, they would have thought they had created it.

The intensity of the moment was unlike either one had ever experienced. They could not resist the moment, nor could they resist each other. That early morning, in the stairwell, Bishop and Mary made love for the first time together, and to both of them what they felt was so incredible that it was like the first time ever.

The whole day they spent together talking and making love. It was like two honeymooners on their first weekend as a married couple off on some exotic location. They were falling in love already. When their twenty-four hour romantic getaway was over, Bishop had to get ready to go with Fighter to Toronto.

"I can't believe that I am saying this right now, but I love you," he said.

Mary was on the exact same page as Bishop. She too had fallen in love. "This is crazy," she said jokingly. "How can we be in love after one night?"

"I've always loved you. You are the only person that I know that has ever really understood me," he said. "The truth is that over all these years, you have been the one constant in my life. You have always been with me through everything that I have been through. I have had life altering things happen to me already, but you and my feelings for you have always stayed with me."

They were standing in front of Fighter's tour bus. Bishop hugged Mary a final time and said, "I'll call you when we get to Toronto. We'll be there two days, then to Cincinnati and Cleveland then on to Chicago and Detroit. When I get back, can I take you out on a date?"

She blushed and laughed and said, "We'll see." Fighter went on their North American tour and Bishop wrote or called Mary nearly every day for three weeks. When he returned, Bishop drove to Baltimore and surprised Mary at her home.

As he walked up to her apartment, he heard noises from inside that rose suspicion. It sounded like a woman screaming. Bishop went directly into warrior mode. He pulled out his pistol that he kept in his waist band and entered the apartment. He could see that no one was in the living room or kitchen, so he quietly moved down the hallway. Once again he heard a muffled scream coming from the bedroom.

With his pistol cocked and leading the way, he slowly opened the door and saw the television was on to a movie. From the corner of his eye he saw Mary coming out of her bathroom. He quickly concealed his gun and Mary jumped when she saw Bishop standing in her doorway. "I heard screaming," he said.

She laughed and said, "I'm sorry, I forgot I left that on while I finished getting ready. How did you get in?"

"The front door was open," he said. He walked up to her and gave her a hug. "Sorry for scaring you. I wanted to surprise you. Were you going out?"

"I thought you were coming back tonight, so I was going to surprise you in New York," she said. "I guess great minds think alike."

It was late autumn and they felt a new change was coming. A change that they both have wanted for a long time. The inseparable relationship that they once had in high school, was picking up right where it left off . . . only now it wasn't two friends, it was two lovers. Bishop moved some things into her apartment and stayed there almost every night for the next eight months.

On Tuesday October 10th 2003, Bishop was sitting at the kitchen table at Mary's apartment when she walked into the room visibly worried. "Are you all right? What's wrong? You look like you've seen a ghost," Bishop said.

"You're sitting down right? Yeah, you're sitting down," she said under her breath. "I'm pregnant," she said. Bishop put his head down into the palms of his hands and then stood up. "Can you say something?" she asked.

He walked over to her, wrapped his arms around her, kissed her and said "I love you, I love you so much."

"So you're happy?" she asked nervously.

"Of course I'm happy, I'm ecstatic!" he said laughing. "This is the best day of my entire life. I'm going to be a Dad . . . I'm going to be a Dad . . . I'm going to be a Dad? I'm going to be a Dad." Bishop could hardly contain his emotions. He was jubilant and scared and proud all wrapped up into one great big ball of emotion. "This is amazing, this is . . . this is awesome," he said. His cell phone began ringing as he expressed his joy. "Hello?" Bishop answered.

"I need to meet you in thirty minutes at Robinson Park. There's a situation." The voice on the phone belonged to Paul Donald. Bishop's emotions instantly changed. He was now concerned with what Donald had to tell him.

"This is such great news honey," Bishop said as he kissed her again. "I have to go take care of some things for the band, I'll be back in a few hours . . . but when I get back, we're gonna celebrate." He grabbed his gun and walked out the door. Five seconds later, he came back inside and passionately kissed her. "I love you." He then finally left. When he found Donald, he could see that whatever was on his mind, had him even more concerned than when Mary told him about the baby.

Before Bishop could even say hello, Donald began informing him of the situation. "The State Department received information that Xavier entered the country through Mobile, Alabama with a falsified passport with the name Gregory Pullman from South Africa. The passport was so good that it didn't come to anyone's attention until another Gregory Pullman from South Africa flew into Boston yesterday. Usually when two people of the same name, flying in from the same foreign country, arrive into the United States, they get red flagged and it comes up in our network of databases. We pulled the surveillance footage from the airport, and got a still image of the first Gregory Pullman, the one who flew into Alabama. Look familiar?" Donald handed Bishop the photo of the man in the airport. Bishop knew it instantly.

"That's him. That's Xavier," Bishop said.

"I'll give you one guess as to where he's headed," Donald said.

"Okay, get me on a plane to Baton Rouge . . . now," Bishop said.

"We already have one waiting . . ." Donald said. "The jet is being fueled as we speak."

The two men jumped into Bishop's car and raced to the airport. Along the way, Bishop got on the phone and called Mary. "Mary, hey . . . listen, I'm gonna be late here so I'm gonna crash at my place tonight. I'll come by in the morning and we'll have breakfast. Is that okay?"

"Sure, that's fine. I was just going to call my mother and let her know about the baby. She is going to flip out," she said.

"Tell you what, if you can wait until tomorrow, then how about you and I go tell her in person?" he said.

"Yeah, that would be better wouldn't it?" she said.

"Okay, well I gotta get going. I'll see you tomorrow. I love you."

"I love you too."

He jumped out of the car and boarded the plane. He took a seat next to a window a few rows down and stared out at the tarmac. "We'll be taking off shortly sir," the captain said.

"Alright, thanks," Bishop responded. "Hey, do you have a pen I can borrow?"

Tuesday,

> *Today, my life begins. A father. I'm going to be somebody's father. Can I keep doing this? Can I keep living both of these lives? It's one thing to be away from my family because of the band, but what if I die doing the other stuff? How could I do that to Mary? How could I do that to my child? I can't. I can't let my kid grow up without a father. I can't do to him, what I had to go through.*

After finishing writing in his journal, Bishop sat back and closed his eyes. He tried to relax and think about a happy future with Mary and his child.

(Hey dad, you want to go play some golf?

Yeah, I would really enjoy that. I'm not letting you beat me this time, though. If you're gonna beat me, it's gonna be because you really beat me.

Oh, you're on. You're going down, old man.

Great drive, son. Now watch how it's done . . . Son? Son where are you? I can't see you. All I see is black. What's happening? Where are you? Son? I can't hear you. I feel like I'm drifting away. What's happening? Son? Son!)

Bishop suddenly was awakened by the jolt of the airplane touching down onto the runway. He was covered in sweat and his heart was racing.

"It was just a dream," he said to himself, with a sigh of relief.

CHAPTER 10

LOOSE ENDS

Bishop arrived in Baton Rouge a little after 12:30 p.m. local time. The car waiting for him at the airport was another BMW. He drove to Carter Petroleum because he knew that had to be where Xavier was headed. Bishop was insistent that the mystery man was now going to get rid of any loose ends that could steer authorities back to him.

When Bishop pulled up to the front gate of the complex, he saw three police cars and an ambulance in front of the main building where Carter's office was located. Bishop was too late. The official report that Bishop would later read was that Jefferson Carter died of head and spinal trauma attributed to a fall down a flight of stairs.

Bishop sped off down the street. He knew that it was a good five miles of open road until civilization, so if he floored it. He thought he might catch up to whomever killed Carter. Bishop's BMW flew down the road. "Come on . . . where are you? You son of a bitch," he said to himself. As he drove down the road, passing nothing but bayou country. He saw, what appeared to be a black or dark blue luxury sedan off in the distance. "Got you," he said.

Bishop pushed the accelerator to the floor. As he approached the car in front of him, a dark blue Mercedes, he could begin to make out features of the driver's head. Bishop was now about two hundred yards away and getting closer. The driver saw him in his mirror and immediately hit his accelerator. The two cars were barreling down the road at over one hundred and thirty miles per hour. The driver turned his head back and aimed his gun at Bishop's car. Bishop instantly recognized the driver as one of the men he previously saw with Xavier. Bishop swerved to the side of the man's car and rammed into the rear left fender, sending the blue sedan sliding out of control. In an instant, the car flipped over on its side and barrel rolled into the woods. Bishop slammed on his brakes and hopped out of his car.

With his gun drawn, Bishop cautiously approached the man's car, which was on its hood with all of the windows busted out. Bishop could hear struggling from inside of the car. He stepped to the driver's side and pointed his gun into the car. "Let me see your hands!" Bishop said. "Show me your hands!" There was no response except for a few gurgling sounds from inside of the car. Bishop peered down and saw a man bleeding all over inside of the car. He was covered in so much blood that Bishop could not clearly see where he was bleeding from. Through the blood splattered carnage, Bishop could still tell that this was not Xavier.

"Tell me his name. Tell me who you work for," Bishop demanded. "You're not going to survive this, you can still die with a clean conscience. Tell me his name." He looked up at Bishop as if he wanted to say something. He started to talk, but when he did, blood oozed from his mouth and he started coughing and laughing. He looked right into Bishop's eyes and smiled, before the life drained from his body. The eerie sight of the man's smile was frozen on his lifeless face like a creepy marionette without its strings.

Bishop pulled the man's body out of the car and searched it for anything useful. He found a passport and a hand written note on a folded napkin that read, "Jefferson Carter, Steven Greyson." That was all, just two names written on a napkin. Bishop now needed to find Steven Greyson. Maybe he would know who the mystery man was.

Bishop left the scene, but first he walked a few yards to an emergency call box on the side of the road and made an anonymous call to 911 informing them of the accident. "Donald, it's Bishop," after hanging up with emergency dispatch he called Paul Donald. "We were too late, Carter's dead."

"Jesus," Donald said.

"Can you get me into the local FBI branch? The guy who took out Carter, had a card with two names written on it. Jefferson Carter was one. The other is someone named Steven Greyson. We gotta get to him before Xavier and the mystery man do," Bishop said.

"Yeah, I'll text you the number and the address. I'll call them right now and inform them that you're coming so they should put you straight through."

"Tell them I'm going to need an address for Greyson," Bishop said.

He hung up the phone and drove back to New Orleans. A few minutes later his phone rang. "This is Bishop," he said.

"Mr. Bishop, this is Special Agent Matthews. I just spoke with Paul Donald. Dr. Steven Greyson is a chemistry professor here at Tulane University. We'll head there now. How far away are you?" Matthews asked.

"Fifteen minutes," Bishop said.

"Okay, we're calling the university now. I'll call you back," Matthews said. He ended the call with Bishop and called the administration building at Tulane. "My name is Special Agent Matthews from the FBI. We have an emergency situation," he said. "I need to know if Dr. Greyson is still on campus . . . uh, huh. No, just call campus security. Have them close that building. No one goes in or out until I get there. I'll be there in . . . eight minutes."

He hung up the phone, and quickly redialed Bishop. "Okay, so we have Greyson. He's still in his classroom. Campus security is going to close off the building," he said.

"Okay, I'm almost there. Don't move in until I'm there," Bishop instructed.

Special Agent Terrance Matthews was just starting his fifth year in the "Bureau," and he was extremely ambitious. He was assigned to the anti-terrorism department of the "Bureau" which handled basically any threat to homeland security within Louisiana.

Bishop pulled up to the campus and found the chemistry labs. He got out of his car and joined Matthews and the other FBI agents. "Greyson is in his classroom preparing for his next class, so there are no students in there right now. The next class starts in twenty minutes," Matthews said.

Bishop and Matthews entered Greyson's room and found him sitting at his desk working on his computer. "Dr. Greyson?" Matthews asked.

"Yes, I'm Steven Greyson," he said.

"FBI, put your hands up where I can see them, doctor," Matthews said. Bishop and the team of FBI agents came into the room with their guns drawn.

"What is this about? What did I do?" Greyson asked.

One of the FBI agents grabbed Greyson and pulled him to his feet. Greyson, a middle-aged man in great physical condition, a physique acquired from years of long distance running and marathon training, was just as mentally astute as he was physically fit. "Step away from your desk," Matthews instructed. Greyson stepped out toward the front of the classroom. He was confused and scared because in his mind, he didn't do anything that warranted an FBI raid, so what could this possibly be about?

An agent instructed Greyson to put his hands on his head while they patted him down for any concealed weapons. When they determined that he wasn't a threat, they sat him down in one of the student's desks at the front of the room. Bishop and Matthews stood in front of him while they questioned him.

"My name is Special Agent Matthews. I'm from the FBI. This is Mr. Bishop; he also works with the United States Government," Matthews said.

"Doctor, we're here because we want to know about your relationship with Jefferson Carter," Bishop said.

"A while back, he came to me about a job offer. He wanted to hire me to help work on a hybrid hydrogen fuel cell," he said.

"How long ago was that?" Matthews asked.

"The initial conversation was about two, two and a half months ago. I met with him a few times and discussed some logistical issues with his plans," Greyson said.

"Such as?" Bishop asked.

"Well, for starters the idea he was proposing is total theory. There has been no substantial, large scale successful test for any practical applications. And also there was the nuclear power issue. From what he told me, I know he had been denied access to any nuclear materials, so making his plan come to fruition was an impossibility," Greyson explained.

"So you stopped talks with Carter after you found out he had been denied access to nuclear materials?" Bishop asked.

"At first, yes. Then a couple of weeks later, he came to see me, and this time he told me that the issue of obtaining the nuclear power we needed was no longer a problem . . . that we could move forward with the project. Well, I wasn't comfortable with the whole thing, so I told them that I was sorry, but I could not help them," he said.

"Them?" Bishop replied. "It wasn't just Carter?"

"No, that last time we spoke, Carter came with another guy. I guess he was his financier or the one who got Carter nuclear access, I'm not real sure. He didn't say much," Greyson said.

"Okay, I want to know everything about this other guy. Tell me everything he said to you," Bishop said excitedly.

"Well, he was actually the one who said that the nuclear power was no longer a problem. He said that that part was taken care of. He didn't specify what that meant, nor did I ask," he said.

"Why didn't you ask?" Matthews asked. Greyson was beginning to get agitated with all of the questions. He was starting to feel like he was on trial.

"You know, I really didn't want to know, to be honest with you," he said. "I didn't trust Carter, and I really didn't get a good vibe from the other guy either. I just didn't want to be any more involved than I already was," he said.

Bishop was leaning his backside against Greyson's personal desk in front. He stood and started pacing in front of Greyson. "Okay, go back to the other guy," Bishop said. "He didn't introduce himself? He didn't tell you his name?"

"No, he did . . . he told me to call him Mr. Androze," he said. "I never got a first name."

"Can you give a description of what he looked like?" Matthews asked.

"I think so, sure," Greyson replied.

"Thank you very much doctor. We're going to need you to come with us to our office so that you can give a formal description. It shouldn't take more than an hour or so, okay?" Matthews said.

They drove back to the FBI office, Bishop couldn't wait to get an actual, legitimate lead on this guy. Bishop and Matthews walked to Matthews' office while Greyson and the illustrator came up with a rendering. As they entered Matthews' office, Bishop said, "We don't have much time. What do you guys have on Jefferson Carter and his business with black market arms dealers?"

Matthews was a little taken back by how much Bishop knew and what he was asking to know. "Well, we know what you know. We know that he was trying to buy high grade uranium, so that he could develop some type of alternative fuel source. He was going to monopolize the market and reap all the benefits. The technology he was working on, if it worked, could revolutionize the entire world. We could finally get over the dependency on fossil fuels."

"Where'd he get the uranium?" Bishop asked.

"Well now that is the $64,000 question. The guy we think he bought it from does not exist . . . at least no one has ever been able to prove he exists," Matthews said. Bishop and Matthews talked for about thirty minutes before the illustrator came into Matthews' office and presented them with the drawing.

"Well gentlemen, here's your suspect," the illustrator said.

Bishop looked at the illustration. He couldn't believe what he was looking at. "Are you positive this is the man you met?" Bishop asked Greyson.

"Yeah, that's him," he said.

Bishop persisted with his questioning. "You're positive? You're sure? This is exactly him, not just kind of similar to what the guy looked like?"

"Yes. I'm sure. That is very close to what the guy looked like," he replied.

Bishop put a hand to his forehead as if to show frustration and disappointment. "What is it?" Matthews asked. "What's wrong?"

"I know this person," Bishop said. Bishop looked at the ground and shook his head. "Damn it," he said under his breath. The man that Greyson had seen and gave an exact description of was none other than Harold Jenkins.

Bishop left the FBI office completely deflated. His friend of more than three years, a man respected by his peers at Interpol and Scotland Yard, was actually (as Bishop was now finding out) a black market weapons dealer and murderer. Bishop left the office and took the last flight back to Maryland. When he got back, he had Donald meet him at the airport. They shook hands as Bishop got off of the plane. Before he even said hello, the first thing out of Bishop's mouth was "Harold Jenkins . . . the son of a bitch we've been looking for is Harold Jenkins. Before I left, I had the FBI call Scotland Yard and Interpol . . ."

"I already know," Donald interrupted. "Five minutes ago, I received a call from Scotland Yard. Jenkins is gone. They're currently checking all of the airports in England and they're checking the Channel Tunnel into France. Bishop . . . Scotland Yard said that when they entered Jenkins' home, they found his wife's body. She had two gunshot wounds to her head. Investigators on the scene said in their estimation, she had been dead at least a week."

"Wait," Bishop said. "Jenkins then knows that I am onto him . . . He knows who I am. He knows about my life. He knows . . . he knows about Mary." Bishop sprinted to his car and broke just about every single driving law in the state of Maryland as he rushed to Mary's apartment. Bishop hit the speed dial to Mary's number. One ring, he looked at the clock, 2:15 a.m. it read. Two rings, "Come on Mary! Answer!" he exclaimed. Three rings, Bishop weaved in and out of the few cars on the highway. Four rings, "ANSWER!!" he shouted. "Answer your phone!"

He was twenty-five minutes away from Mary's apartment; he made it in ten. All along the way he repeatedly hit redial on his phone; each time he got voicemail. He pulled up to the apartment, slammed on the brakes, put it in park and jumped out. He ran through the apartment complex and up to Mary's second floor apartment. He slowed himself down as he reached the door. He stood there at the door for a second and collected himself. He took a deep breath, grasped the doorknob and started to turn it. It was still locked. A small bit of comfort and relief came over Bishop.

He pulled his key from his pocket and his gun from the holster in his waist band. He feared that if Jenkins sent someone to kill Mary, they could still be inside. He searched the apartment and promptly went to Mary's bedroom. He opened the door and found her seemingly peacefully in her bed.

He went up to her and gently put his hand on her forehead to make sure she was still alive. His heart pounded so hard, he could feel it hitting his rib cage. It beat and pounded so fast and rhythmically, that it could've been mistaken for a drum solo at a rock concert. She rolled over and continued to sleep on her side.

A very relieved Bishop looked up across the room and noticed that the bathroom door was closed. He softly rose to his feet and approached the door. He opened the door and scanned the room. It was empty. The rest of the night, Bishop sat in a chair in the living room to keep guard for any possible intruders. As the rising sunlight beamed through the blinds, Bishop began contemplating his life. His job had now become hazardous to his personal life.

"What the hell have I done? What the hell have I gotten Mary into?"

CHAPTER 11

AGONY IN THE WORKPLACE

The morning came and just like he promised, Bishop was there for breakfast with Mary. She woke up to an alarm clock that most people would love to have, the aroma of fresh ground coffee brewing in the kitchen. She opened eyes with early morning disdain, but with a smile for that she knew that Bishop had returned. She got out of bed and put on one of Bishop's long sleeve shirts, the soft cotton kind that feels so comfortable that you never want to take it off. She went into the kitchen and found Bishop standing over the stove. He was making heart shaped pancakes for breakfast. "Hello stranger," she said.

Bishop turned and couldn't help but smile at her. For him, seeing her standing there was perfection. The world was perfect because he had her in his life. She was what made good things great and difficult times into an after-thought. "My God . . . you're even more beautiful than I remember," he said.

She laughed and said, "You just saw me yesterday."

"It was a long day . . .," he said, "and you're still beautiful." He kissed her and she sat down at the kitchen table.

They sat and ate breakfast together and as far as Bishop was concerned, they could have stayed there forever. He was even more conflicted with what he should do. He knew that Jenkins and Xavier were now a major threat, not only to the world, but more intimately, they were a threat to Mary and himself. This had to end. If Bishop wanted to have some sort of normalcy with Mary, he needed to end things with Jenkins.

"Mary?" Bishop started to say something, but paused because he wasn't sure what he was going to say. "There's something . . ."

Mary's telephone rang, interrupting Bishop. "I'm sorry," she said as she stood up to pick up the phone. "Hello?" Mary answered. There was a long pause, and her face turned as white as the plates on the table. She dropped the phone and sunk down to the floor.

"Mary!" Bishop jumped out of his seat and grabbed Mary. "What's wrong? Who was that?"

Mary started crying uncontrollably. Bishop tried everything to comfort her. "Mary, please . . . what's wrong? You're scaring me."

She raised her head. Her face was covered in tears. "My mother died. She was murdered," she said.

Bishop fell back onto his back side. He knew what happened. He knew this had to be Xavier and Jenkins. His worst fears were coming true. The people he loved and cared for, were now being killed because of who he was, and what he did. Bishop didn't say a word except, "I'm so sorry." He grabbed her and held her there on the kitchen floor. They sat there and grieved for the greater part of an hour, not saying anything. Bishop just sat there and held her. What can one really say in a situation like that? What magical words can be uttered to make things better? The fact is, there are no words. Sometimes life is simply hell.

After Mary showed signs that she was calming down, Bishop said to her. "We should go to the hospital. One of us will have to identify your mom." He hated himself for having to say that. That sentence was the worst thing that ever came out of Bishop's mouth. He knew that this was his fault, or at least that was his view on the situation.

Bishop helped Mary change and then they drove to the hospital where Mary's mother was taken. The whole way to the hospital, Mary just stared out the window. She never said a word and the only sign of life came when Bishop reached over and grabbed her hand. She squeezed his hand and held on for the rest of the twenty minute drive.

At the hospital, the doctors told Mary that they needed her to identify her mother. Bishop said to her, "Are you okay? Can you do this?"

"Yeah . . . I . . . I'm okay. I can do this," she said.

"I'm very sorry for your loss," the doctor said.

"Do you want me to be with you while you do this?" Bishop asked.

"Please," she responded. Mary and Bishop entered the room and Mary was able to see her mom one last time and say goodbye. After a few minutes, the doctor came back and told Mary that she needed to fill out some paperwork.

Bishop said to Mary, "I'll just wait for you out here." He was referring to the waiting room. Mary went to a receptionist's desk and Bishop started walking to the waiting room. As he was walking away, he changed directions and went to the doctor who examined the body. "Excuse me, doctor," Bishop said. "I was wondering if you could tell me a little more about what happened. I know that Mary is too distraught right now to think about it, but I think we should know exactly what happened."

The doctor explained that Mary's mother had been beaten with a blunt object and then strangled. Aside from those initial wounds, the doctor said that they would know more after an autopsy. "Are there any police officers still here who were at the crime scene?" Bishop asked.

"I think so," the doctor said. "The investigator was looking for you guys before you got here, but I think he left momentarily. He said that he would be back shortly . . . oh, there he is right there." The doctor looked behind Bishop and pointed to the police investigator walking toward them.

He was mildly heavy set and was wearing a light brown suit. He was holding a cup of coffee and eating a donut as he approached Bishop and introduced himself. Still chewing on his last bite of the donut, he said, "Hi, I'm Detective North. Are you a relative of the deceased?" he asked.

Bishop was not very happy with the Detective's lack of tactfulness toward the situation. "No, I'm a friend of Mrs. Wilson's daughter. She's filling out some paperwork with the hospital. Can you tell me what happened?"

"I'm sorry, if you're not a relative, I can't disclose any information at this time without consent of a relative," North said.

Just then, Mary walked into the room where they were all standing. "Well, I'll leave you to the Detective. I'm sorry again for your loss," the doctor said to Mary as he walked away.

"Mary Wilson?" the detective asked.

"Yes, I'm Mary Wilson," she said.

Their conversation lasted forever it seemed to Mary. She struggled to answer the detective's questions. "When did you last see your mom? . . . What did you talk about? . . . Is there anyone you believe that wanted to hurt your mom?" The whole time, Bishop stood by her side and held her hand for support. Finally, the detective said, "Okay Mary, I think I have enough right now. We can finish doing this later." The detective shook their hands and starting walking away.

Bishop said to Mary, "I'll be right back, okay?" He jogged after the detective and stopped him outside the hospital. "Detective," Bishop said. North turned around. "Can I ask you a few things?"

"Go ahead Mr. Bishop," he said.

"Was there a struggle?" Bishop asked.

"The evidence indicates that she did not struggle. It looks like someone attacked her from behind . . . she suffered the first blow to the head and was probably incapacitated," he said. "I really don't have time for this Mr. Bishop, nor should I be discussing any of this. This is an open investigation."

Bishop knew he wasn't going to get much from North. He went back inside and continued to comfort Mary. They left the hospital and went back to Mary's apartment and all Mary wanted to do was lay in bed. Bishop did some domestic things around the apartment, like dishes and laundry. Around lunch time, he woke her up and brought her a sandwich that she ended up not eating. A few hours later, Bishop woke her up and asked if she wanted some dinner.

"Okay, give me a few minutes okay? I want to wash my face," she said. Bishop could see that she had been crying.

"Okay," he said. "I'll get it started, come on out when you're ready."

They sat across from each other in silence the entire time. Bishop knew what Mary was going through and knew that if she didn't feel like talking, he wasn't going to force conversation. She was there for him twice when he lost his parents, now the tables were turned and he was going to do whatever she needed to get through the anguish.

After dinner, Mary told him "I think I just want to go to sleep."

"Okay," Bishop said. "I think you'll feel a little better in the morning."

Bishop waited for Mary to fall asleep and then he went to her mother's house to look at the crime scene. He pulled up to her house and saw the yellow crime scene tape blocking the front door. He had taken Mary's spare key to her mother's house and unlocked the door. It was an eerie feeling as he walked inside. He was surprisingly okay seeing her mother at the hospital, but when he walked into her mother's house he suddenly had memories of his own parents and felt sadness all the way to his core.

There was a dry blood stain on the carpet in the living room the size of a dinner plate. He also found a small blood splatter on the wall, so he determined which way she was facing and which direction the killer approached her from behind. He examined the doors and windows, trying to determine where the killer entered the house. He noticed a small amount of paint chipped off under a window in the bedroom. The killer must have pried open the window and entered through the bedroom. Bishop scanned the living room area and tried to figure out where the killer must have hid. He turned his head and focused on the closet in the entryway to the house. He walked over and turned around to see the point of view from the closet to the living room.

Mary's mother must not have been home when the killer got there. He must have waited in the closet for her to come home and when she walked past him he must have attacked her from behind. Bishop approached the closet and opened the door. At first glance, it looked normal. A few coats, a vacuum cleaner, a few small boxes up on the shelf occupied the closet. Bishop moved some things around and found nothing.

He stood there facing the closet, evaluating the situation. Still puzzled, Bishop went into the closet and closed the door. He wanted to get the perspective of the killer. There was no light in the closet so he could not see anything. He was ready to give up and he opened the door. When the door opened and some light came in, Bishop noticed a folded up piece of paper taped to the wall of the closet near the door frame.

Bishop unfolded the paper and read a single letter, "X." It was Xavier. Bishop didn't need to find the note to know who killed Mary's mother, but now that he had confirmation he was determined to find Xavier. He was not going to stop until Xavier was dead. Now knowing that Xavier was killing everyone around Bishop, he had to tell Mary she was in danger . . . and why.

In the morning, Bishop waited for Mary to wake up so that he could have the unbelievably difficult conversation with her, an impossible conversation really, but it had to be done. He feared that she would never forgive him for possibly putting her and her mother in danger, but the time for fearing such things was over. The threat was real, and Mary was in danger. Mary came out of her room and Bishop greeted her with a cup of coffee. "How are you feeling?" he asked.

"I'm okay," she said. "Thank you for everything, I appreciate it."

Bishop's heart sank into his stomach. Little did she know, she was actually thanking him for allowing her mother to be murdered.

"I have to talk to you," he said. "I have to tell you something about my life that you don't know. What I have to tell you, is going to be difficult to hear. You're not going to like what I have to say, and . . . and I pray that you can forgive me for what I am about to say."

"What? What is it?" she asked. She really couldn't take anymore heartbreak. She was already fragile enough.

"Since I left the military, I've still been working for the government," he explained. "I can't tell you everything about what I do, but I've been working for the government and the man that . . .(he couldn't stomach the reality of the situation) hurt your mom, was really coming after me."

"What? . . . what? What are you saying?" she asked. Her heart was pounding and she was struggling to wrap her head around what he was telling her.

"I've been working with the government in an anti-terrorism agency and I've been investigating someone. This person . . . killed your mom . . . as a message to me," he said.

Mary cut him off again, "Message? What do you mean message? What are you . . . what are you talking about?"

He started to tell her that they needed to go somewhere and hide for a while. "Mary, you're in danger . . ." Just as he started speaking, she slapped him.

"You son of a bitch!" she said. She slapped him again. He didn't try to defend himself in any way. "You son of a bitch. How can you do that? How can you put us through this? She's dead . . . she's dead because of you, YOU! Because of YOU! You bastard." She started crying uncontrollably and Bishop couldn't do anything to comfort her. "I want you out. Get out!" she screamed.

"Mary, it's not safe for you here . . ."

"GET OUT!!" The slap across his face bruised him almost immediately, but the physical bruise on his face paled in comparison to the bruise on his heart. He hadn't felt anything like it since the death of his father.

She wasn't going to listen to him. She stood up and shoved him toward the door. He could clearly see she needed space away from him, away from everything that reminded her of him, and he cared enough for her to give her that space. He knew that she was in danger, but in that moment his emotions as a boyfriend overshadowed his rational thinking. He walked out the door and called Donald. He told him that he needed immediate surveillance of Mary's house. He needed Donald to get twenty-four hour patrol, to make sure Xavier wouldn't kill her next. Bishop needed to find Jenkins and he needed to find him quickly.

The days following were much of the same. Bishop tried to talk to Mary, but she wasn't giving him any opportunities to do so. She was feeling resentment and extreme sorrow and those two emotions don't come with an on/off switch.

Several months passed, and nothing had changed. Bishop devoted all of his time trying to find Jenkins, all the while, doing whatever he could to make things okay between him and Mary.

After an obsessive seven and a half months of tracking possible leads on Jenkins' whereabouts, Bishop finally caught a break. Bishop tracked Jenkins to Panama City, Panama. Jenkins was easier to find than Xavier, only because of Bishop's past relationship with Jenkins. He could anticipate his moves. He figured that Jenkins was using an alias, and was very good at disappearing. After-all, Jenkins was hiding in plain sight the whole time he was buying and selling weapons on the black market. Bishop took a chance and searched for the alias Jenkins used with Dr. Greyson . . . Androze.

He searched all incoming passport checks in Paris, Berlin, Lisbon, Bangkok and Hong Kong, all of the possible locations where Jenkins could have fled. Bishop came up empty. Then he remembered a conversation the two men had about a year ago. Jenkins told Bishop a story of when Jenkins was in Her Majesty's Navy and for six months he was stationed in Panama City, Panama. He said that that was his dream retirement spot and that he planned on buying a place on the beach about ten miles south of Panama City.

The skyline of Panama City looked more like an American metropolis than a common Central American city. Panama City is one of the most affluent cities in Latin America. It's a major port for international trade, which has attracted all sorts of major corporations. It's a location that someone could disappear to or from quite easily. They could go down into South America or to the west into Asia.

The road to Jenkins' beach front home was covered by a canopy of palm trees and tropical rainforest. The house was at the bottom of a hill at the base of a cliff. The view was straight off a post card. Jenkins, who was using the alias Harry Androze, was driving his Mercedes-Benz SLS AMG convertible and smoking a Cuban cigar. He pulled up to his house, which was guarded by an eight foot solid wooden gate. The gate was attached to an equally tall stone wall that surrounded the house. The circular drive way wrapped around a large Koi pond and fountain. Each time Jenkins entered or exited his car, a flurry of orange, black and white stirred the pond.

Mayan statues shipped in from southern Mexico, sat in front of the house. The front doors were tall double French doors made out of a reddish ash wood. As Jenkins walked inside, he passed a tall mirror that stretched from the black marble flooring to the ceiling. He put his keys down in a small bowl made of jade that was on a long table next to a coat stand.

The faint, but compelling sound of a gun being cocked, startled Jenkins. "You're getting sloppy at your old age Harold," a voice said.

Bishop walked up behind Jenkins. He was waiting for him in the living room area that was adjacent to the entryway. A wall separated the two rooms, so Jenkins could not see Bishop. "Keep your hands where I can see them. You used the same alias you used with Dr. Greyson in New Orleans."

"I knew I should've taken care of that quicker," Jenkins said. Jenkins turned around and faced Bishop. Bishop had his Beretta M9 pointed right at Jenkins. "Bishop, listen . . . about Mary's mother, it had to be done. It was strictly business . . ." BANG!! A shot rang out and Jenkins fell to the floor grabbing his right knee. "Damn it!" he said in pain.

"Don't you dare talk about her, Harold," Bishop said.

"Aghhh!! Do you have any idea how much this hurts?" Jenkins asked.

"You know, I thought that I might have trouble doing this, seeing how we were friends and all, but as it turns out . . ." BANG!!! Another shot echoed through the house. "This is actually quite easy," Bishop said as he shot Jenkins in the elbow. Jenkins was screaming and writhing in pain on the marble floor. "Now this is the part where you tell me where Xavier is, Harold," Bishop said.

He was now pointing his gun at Jenkins' stomach. "I don't know," he answered angrily. BANG! Bishop shot Jenkins in the hand. He was trying for a clean shot through the center of his hand, but his carelessness and total disregard for Jenkins resulted in Bishop shooting his left hand between the thumb and index finger. The shot left the thumb almost severed. It was barely hanging on by skin and muscle. "Aghhh Ahhh!!! I swear I don't know," he screamed.

"I'm getting pretty tired of this Harold," Bishop said. Bishop didn't care if Jenkins lived or died, as long as he could tell him how to find Xavier. He pointed the gun at Jenkins' stomach.

"He contacts me via text message on a pre-paid cell phone. The number changes each time and he uses a different name each time he starts a new account. Believe me, I checked this guy out. This guy knows what he's doing," Jenkins explained.

"When was the last time you had contact?" Bishop asked. Jenkins said nothing. He looked at Bishop and shook his head no. Bishop pressed the gun into Jenkins' testicles. "When?" he demanded.

"A week ago. A week ago," he replied. Bishop pulled the gun back and searched Jenkins for a gun. Bishop stood up and walked away. Jenkins was rolling around on the floor, trying to move. He caught a glimpse of the massive pool of his own blood that he was laying in. "Oh my God. Oh my God," he said. He was beginning to panic at the realization that death was not far off. Bishop returned with Jenkins' cell phone and dropped it on his chest.

"Call him," he said. Jenkins didn't move or reply. He just stared at Bishop. In a moment of anger and frustration, Bishop shot Jenkins in the stomach. "CALL him!" he repeated.

Jenkins was going into shock from the gunshots. Blood began seeping out of his mouth. He started coughing, causing more blood to pour out. "I'm a dead man either way Bishop," he said. Jenkins started sliding across the floor in the dark crimson colored pool, trying to get away from Bishop. Bishop started pacing around because he was getting tired of listening to Jenkins. "But I am not going to be a dead snitch," he said. Bishop had turned his back long enough for Jenkins to get to a gun he had hidden in the drawer of the table in the entryway.

Bishop turned back around, Jenkins was pointing the gun at him. "Shit," Bishop said as he ducked behind a large chair. Jenkins wanted Bishop to shoot him, but since he took cover instead of shooting, Jenkins turned the gun on himself.

CHAPTER 12

PEACE AT LAST?

B ishop was now back to square one. He had no leads to go on to find Xavier. With Jenkins dead, Bishop didn't know if Xavier would still come for Bishop and Mary, or if he would ever hear from him ever again. Bishop wasn't content with the idea of the latter. Bishop was now devoted to finding Xavier, before Xavier found him first.

Bishop searched Jenkins' house for any clue to Xavier's whereabouts. He looked for anything, a receipt, a note, ticket stub, anything that could point him in the right direction. Alas, he found nothing.

"Surely there must be something," he said. "He hired the guy, there must be something here." He searched the house again, starting with the bedroom. He walked down a well-lit hallway that was illuminated by a series of skylights in the ceiling. Through the glass, Bishop could see over-hanging tree limbs, giving shade to the house. Photographs of Jenkins with friends and family members hung on the wall.

The bedroom was lavish, just like the rest of the house. A large four post bed sat against the wall in the center of the room. Two nightstand tables sat on either side of the bed. A large oak armoire stood across from the bed. Bishop tried to open the cabinet, but it was locked shut by a small lock on the front. There was a large penknife on one of the nightstands. Bishop grabbed it and tried to open the lock. He attempted this for about two minutes before trying to wedge the penknife in between the doors and pry it open. After yet another failed attempt, Bishop's final try at opening the doors was the quickest, yet crudest way. He pulled out his Beretta M9, held a pillow in front of the barrel to suppress the sound and shot it open.

The inside of the cabinet revealed a series of shelves with papers stacked neatly on each one. Tax returns, bank statements, even some documents from Jenkins' retirement from military service were in the cabinet, but nothing in any of those documents indicated any kind of relationship or connection to Xavier.

At the very back of the top shelf of the cabinet, Bishop found a Polaroid photograph. In the photo, there were two men in military uniforms standing over a large stack of what Bishop perceived to be heroin or cocaine. On the back of the Polaroid, "Belize, 1982" was written. He immediately recognized one of the men as Jenkins, only about twenty years younger. The other man, Bishop wasn't quite sure who it was. Bishop stared at the Polaroid for several minutes straight, trying to figure out who the other person was.

Finally, the face became clear to Bishop. The man with Jenkins was none other than Xavier. Bishop put the picture in his pocket and continued to search the house. There was nothing else in the house that linked Jenkins to Xavier, only the Polaroid and he didn't even know what the meaning of the photo was. Bishop walked back to Jenkins' body. From the massive pool of blood on the marble floor, it looked to Bishop as if Jenkins had completely bled out, or at least that is what it looked like.

Bishop stood there for a moment and remembered Jenkins the way he thought he knew him, as a friend. "Good bye old friend," he said. "Sorry it had to be like this." For the moment, Bishop forgot the fact that Jenkins was at least partially responsible for killing Mary's mother. When the moment had passed, Bishop dropped a match onto the floor, igniting the gasoline that he had siphoned from Jenkins' Mercedes. The place lit up quickly as Bishop drove away.

The flight back to the United States was a long one for Bishop. The prospect of uncertainty was weighing on his mind. Not knowing what his life was to be like with Mary and his son, he did know that his priority was with them first and Falcon second. Nevertheless, finding Xavier was in the back of his mind.

The private jet landed at Andrews Air Force Base in Maryland. As usual, Bishop anticipated Paul Donald to be waiting for him on the tarmac. As the plane taxied along the runway to its final destination, Bishop could see out of the window the absence of his commanding officer. He got off the plane and walked to his car that was waiting for him and hopped inside.

As Bishop settled into his car, he checked his phone for messages. Forty-seven missed calls and thirty-one messages, almost all from the same number, Mary's number. He immediately called back and got her voicemail. He listened to the messages. Mary was calling to tell him that she was going into labor. This was alarming to Bishop because Mary wasn't due for three more weeks. The messages and missed calls started coming in two days prior and the last came eleven hours ago. Bishop had missed the birth of his child. He called the hospital in Baltimore and asked if she was still there and if she was okay. He was informed that she was still there and that the baby was under observation.

He raced to the hospital, completely ignoring red lights and stop signs. When he got there, he found Mary's room and stood outside the door for several minutes, thinking about what he would say to her. After several minutes of pacing in the hallway, he built up enough courage to go in and face Mary.

She was sleeping in her bed when he went inside. He walked up to her bed and sat down in a chair that was next to her. He sat there watching her sleep for an hour. She looked so peaceful sleeping there. He knew his child was in the nursery, and he wanted to meet the child for the first time, but he wanted to stay by Mary's side for just a little while longer. He wanted to see her first, and apologize for not being there.

Finally, Mary woke up and saw Bishop sitting next to her. At first sight, her face softened with a smile, but when she remembered that he wasn't there for her on the most important day of her life, her face saddened. She said nothing to him, only turning her head the other way in disgust. Mary would have been okay with Bishop's military obligations had he been honest with her about it. She would have been able to forgive him for not being there, had she known that he was facing an obligation to his country, but instead he lied to her . . . and lying was something that she had trouble forgiving.

"Nothing I can say, can right the wrong I did," he said. "If you'll let me, I promise I will be there for you. I love you Mary. I'm so sorry that I lied to you. I never meant to hurt you. I want to be in your life. I want to be a father. You're the only woman I've ever loved Mary. I'm so sorry. Please forgive me . . ."

"I don't know if I can forgive you," she said, cutting him off. "If you're serious, I'm glad to hear that you want to be a father."

"And I am, I am," he said.

"But what you did was so hurtful. I'm going to need time to get past this. You're going to have to prove that I can trust you. Right now, I don't trust you. I've lost faith in you. I don't know how you get that back," she said.

"I'll do whatever it takes," he said.

Mary paused and looked at him for a moment. She could see it in his face the sadness and disappointment he was feeling. She could see the guilt and remorse. "Would you like to meet your son?" she asked. Bishop's heart swelled with joy. He began crying.

"Yes . . . God yes," he said. Bishop helped Mary into a wheelchair and pushed her to the nursery, for she was still physically exhausted from the nine hour birth. They arrived at the window where parents and family could see their new born children. Bishop identified him immediately. He was seven pounds, nine ounces of pure joy for Bishop.

"I know we hadn't decided on a name yet, but I was thinking Sam, after your father," she said. Bishop was choked up with emotion. All he could do to respond was laugh through his tears and nod his head an emphatic, yes. The next couple of weeks, Bishop never left Mary's side. He did everything for her, drawing her bath, making dinner AND doing the dishes, massaging her back and shoulders. Dishes and laundry, vacuuming and mopping, all of the day to day chores, Bishop took care of them. He even began to turn the second bedroom into a nursery. It was while he was in the home repair store, surveying the paint options for the baby's room that Bishop really had an epiphany of sorts. A realization of how he should be living his life.

It was almost three weeks after Bishop had returned home when he got the phone call he was dreading.

"I trust that you found what you were looking for," the voice said.

Bishop recognized the voice immediately. It was Paul Donald. "Where were you when I got back from Panama, Paul?"

"I'm sorry, I had to be in a meeting at the Pentagon," he said. "I had to explain why my best agent was making an unscheduled, overnight trip to Central America."

"What did you tell them?" Bishop asked.

"That as far as I know, I didn't know anything about any trip to Central America . . . however, if one of my agents did go to Central America, I'm sure that our national security would be more secure because of it, and discretion would be exhibited to the utmost level," Donald responded.

"You really are good at your job, aren't you Paul?" Bishop asked. "The amount of bullshit you can spew is obscene. Thank you Paul." Bishop's voice expressed his genuine gratitude for covering him as he thanked Donald. Falcon did have high level top secret status, but like any other agency they still had to follow protocol. An unsanctioned assassination was not going to be looked upon favorably by Donald's superiors at the Pentagon, so he was covering for himself, just as much as he was covering up for Bishop.

"Are the problems alleviated?" Donald asked.

"Jenkins is no longer a problem," he said. "Xavier is still in play." Bishop and Donald had to talk in code on their cell phones for security purposes, even though the coded dialogue was fairly easy to decipher. "Quite frankly Paul, right now I am not concerned with Xavier. Right now I am more concerned with being a father to my son."

There was a long pause on the phone. "What are you saying?" Donald asked.

"I'm saying that I don't know. I don't know if I want to be a part of Falcon anymore. I'm saying that I don't know if I can leave on a moment's whim, and not tell my family when I'll be back. I don't even know if fighting for my country is a top priority for me anymore."

Finally, Donald responded "Are you giving me your resignation, because I am not accepting it. You're too good at this Bishop. If you need time to adjust, and make things right at home, then that's fine. I can accept that. I can't just let you walk away from this." Bishop didn't know what to say. He sat there on the receiving end of the phone, truly not knowing what to say or do.

"I should also tell you Bishop, the final report of the explosion at Jefferson Carter's office came in. The remains of three individuals were identified, none of which were Carter." Bishop couldn't give him an answer right then. He wasn't sure what to do, not even learning that Jefferson Carter could still be alive was enough to pull him away from his family. He contemplated for days and those even turned into weeks.

"How do I fix this? How do I correct the wrongs that I have committed? Is there anything that I can do to repair my own psyche?" He tore himself up thinking about the fate of his own soul, his own mind. He had failed the one person left in his life who loved him.

Bishop knew that the harm he had done to Mary was probably so abominable that he risked losing her forever. He needed to take action. He needed to change his life immediately. If things were going to get better, Bishop had to make a decision to get his priorities in the right order. At the very top of his priorities was becoming a better man, a better husband, and the best father he could be.

The fate of Fighter and most of all, the fate of Falcon was up in the air. At that moment, Bishop wasn't concerned or worried about making the world a better place, and certainly not concerned with playing music. All that he was concerned with, was making his own life a better place.

For several days, Bishop stayed by Mary's side. He did everything and anything she asked of him, he even went above and beyond and did the little things that she didn't mention but he anticipated she'd need or ask for . . . a regular "Mr. Mom."

CHAPTER 13

WORST OF THE WORST

Several weeks passed since Bishop's phone call with Paul Donald and Bishop wasn't any more decided on what to do about his future with Falcon. He was beginning to be quite accustomed to domestic life. Though he was no longer living with Mary, Bishop did rent an apartment in the same complex and was spending as much time as possible with her and their son. To help himself become a better person, Bishop continued writing in his journal every day about his thoughts on what he needed to do better.

Friday, June 12

> *It takes a long time and a lot of work to regain trust from someone that you have deceived. In fact, there is a very real chance that the person you have deceived may never fully trust you again. Though I am not at peace with this per say, I do accept it. I also accept that the rest of my life will have to be devoted to being honest with Mary. I can no longer live in lies and half-truths. I don't want my son to view me like that, nor do I want to honor the memory of my parents in that way by tarnishing their namesake. There is no honor in living in lies.*

Monday, June 15

> *I spent the weekend with Mary. It was very nice and things seem to be getting back to normal. I can sense more comfort between us. Mary seems to be less consumed with hurt and disappointment. This is a very comforting sign for us, especially for me. However, this gradual rise back to normalcy is accompanied with stress and frustration for me as well. Even though I am blessed to have a great and exciting life with Fighter, I can't shake this constant feeling in me. I try filling this gaping hole inside of me with both the fast-lane rock and roll life and the mundane civilian monotony. But, no matter what I seem to do, my life doesn't quite seem complete. The past few days I have begun thinking about returning to Falcon. I hope Mary understands this is something that I need to do.*

Bishop was nervous about talking to Mary about his feelings with regard to going back to Falcon, even though it was the truth. Little did he know, Mary had been anticipating that conversation for quite some time. Bishop apologized for what he needed to do. "I'm sorry for putting you through this, but before I do this, I need to have your support."

Because Mary knew this day would come, there was no surprise. And because she loved Bishop, she was able to be at peace with supporting him. "I knew this day would come, and I understand this is the life that you need to live." They talked for the rest of the day. Bishop was amazed by Mary's grace towards his dichotomy. But . . . as it turns out, the truth did set him free.

Bishop made the call to Donald. "I'm going after Carter," Bishop said. "He may be the only one who can lead me to Xavier." The call was short and to the point. Donald didn't need any explanation, and Bishop was not about to give any. The point was made clear: Bishop was back, and that was what Paul Donald cared about.

Donald sent Bishop an intelligence report, citing all of Jefferson Carter's known business associates, financial and real estate holdings, and residences. The report also underlined William Carter, Jefferson Carter's brother who ran the Banca d'Italia. In the report, it said that William had a large estate in Rome. This must be where Jefferson was hiding, he thought. But why did Carter fake his own death? And why did Xavier and Jenkins help him fake his death?

Fighter was no longer touring, so Bishop didn't have to worry about his obligations to the band. He would have time to finally put an end to Carter and Xavier. Donald had Bishop drive to Langley, Virginia to the CIA central office. Bishop had only seen it depicted in movies. Being there in person was even more surreal than he had dreamed it to be.

As he drove to the complex, he was stopped at numerous security check-points. Donald had given him clearance to visit, but the security was still on high alert. Bishop didn't know if this was typical protocol, or if the heightened security was do to a national security terror threat. Either way, Bishop was thoroughly impressed with all of the high-tech precautions.

Paul Donald was waiting in front of one of the main buildings. They went inside and made their way through another series of security check-points before coming to a large room filled with desks manned by researchers and analysts.

"Quite the set-up you got here," Bishop said.

"We have twenty-five analysts, working ten hour shifts, twenty-four hours a day, three hundred sixty-five days a year . . . three hundred and sixty-six in leap years," Donald said. "That's just in this office, alone. They're all analyzing and recording every lead that comes to us regarding possible terror threats in the eastern United States, primarily threats involving technological devices such as explosive devices or even in cyber space. One of the fastest growing terrorist threats to western societies isn't that of a nuclear or chemical device, it's ones and zeros . . . binary code. The idea is possible and the threat is real that someone could hack into any computer and take control of whatever the system is running on that computer, Cyber terrorism, if you will. For example, if someone gained access to the network controlling the simple numbers on the NASDAQ or New York Stock Exchange, they could cripple our economy in one day by driving up or dropping values. Or say someone gained access to one of the networks of an air traffic controller, they could start crashing commercial airliners."

"I was under the impression that most of these types of cyber terrorist threats were thought to be a little exaggerated," Bishop said.

"Hey, you know it sounds crazy but after 9/11, the fear of something like that actually happening is very real," Donald said. "And of course there is always the biggest of all major computer terrorist threats, and that is if someone gains access to a network that would launch one of our own nuclear bombs. The further we progress into the technological era, the threat of someone building a nuclear bomb and using it against us is only one way of attacking us. The threat now could be that someone figures out a way of using our own nuclear bombs against us. Like in the movie War Games."

A young man, tall in stature, was standing behind Bishop, listening to the conversation. "True, that it's like War Games, but I like to think of it as like Die Hard 2," he said. Bishop turned to look at who was speaking. Bishop stood at a respectable six foot one, and when he looked at the young man, Bishop had to look up to make eye contact.

"Who are you?" Bishop asked. There was a slight annoyance in his voice.

"Tyler Harper," the young man said. "It's nice to finally meet you Bishop. I feel like I've known you forever. We've been keeping constant tabs on all of our operatives. With regard to someone seizing air traffic control systems via hacking into a computer network, the idea that you could use airliners as weapons is a bit of a fallacy. You can't hijack a plane remotely. If the idea is to crash an airliner into a specific building or area, you have to do it the old fashioned way of physically taking control of the cockpit. However, if simply crashing a commercial airliner with hundreds of innocent people on board is your objective, then that threat is real."

"That's quite disturbing . . . oh, and just call me Bishop," Bishop said. He turned back and looked at Donald. "So, what does any of this have to do with Jefferson Carter or Xavier?"

"Well, none of this does, but Harper here has also been working on Carter as well," Donald said.

"The day that Carter bought that uranium, we've been keeping an eye him," Harper said. "We've been paying an especially close look at Carter's brother . . ."

"William Carter," Bishop interrupted. "The banker in Rome. I was the one who first got you guys that intel."

"That's correct," Harper said. "We believe that Jefferson Carter has been lying low at his brother's estate in Rome." Harper pulled up some images on a screen of a man walking into Carter's home. The images were side by side with a picture of Jefferson Carter as a reference. "We believe this is Jefferson Carter." The pictures showed a side profile of a man that resembled Jefferson Carter.

"That's him," Bishop said. "That's definitely him. So what do we do from here? I mean, what's the CIA prepared to do about bringing him in?"

"Let's go talk in my office," Donald said to Bishop. The two men walked across the room and into a sound-proof glass walled office. Donald's office was a typical looking office with a large black desk, a few filing cabinets, and a small sofa. The one difference that made Donald's office different from the average civilian office was the smart glass wall that, at the flip of a switch, changed from clear to opaque.

"What's going on, Paul?" Bishop asked. "Why haven't you guys moved on Carter? Why haven't I been given any intel until now? You owe it to me to tell me what's going on. What aren't you telling me?"

Donald opened one of his filing cabinets and removed a file. He placed it on his desk and sat down. Bishop sat down in a chair across from Donald. "I've been instructed by my superiors to limit your knowledge and resources with this case. I know what you have been through already. I know what sacrifices you've made to bring down Jenkins and Carter, believe me I know. If I had it my way, you'd be leading this thing and quite frankly, I have no doubts that you would've already finished this." Donald opened up the file and placed it in front of Bishop on the table. He then placed a stack of blank paper next to it. "Speaking for myself and the top brass above me, we have nothing but the utmost respect and gratitude for you, and I would never suspect that you would be the kind of person to interfere or try to take control of this investigation yourself. I mean, no one would ever suspect you to be the kind of person to walk out of here with classified documents if you had the opportunity to do so. No one would suspect that."

Bishop saw the obvious opportunity that Donald was presenting to him. As Donald got up, turned his back and walked around the room as he talked, Bishop switched the documents with the blank pages and put the documents inside the waistband of his pants. It was one long time friend, helping another. Donald was never the kind of person to fully see the need for protocol when a solution to a problem was already in place. He knew that Bishop not only deserved to be a part of this mission, but he also knew that he was the best man for the job.

Bishop stood up and approached Donald. "Thank you Paul," he said. "If there's any way you guys could need my help, I'll be there." They shook hands and Bishop left the building quickly, for he knew that if he got caught with those documents he would be arrested for sure.

He got into his car and drove about five miles down the road to a rest stop. He pulled over and stopped so he could read the classified documents.

<u>Classified</u>   *3 August 2012*

SUBJECT: Oil Tycoon Jefferson Carter Suspected of Buying Stolen Uranium

Reporting Special Agent Kyle Bishop suggests that Jefferson Carter has purchased stolen Turkish uranium. Special Agent Bishop pursued courier suspected of transporting $75,000 to a suspected Black Market arms dealer of unknown identity to eastern Pakistan where Special Agent Bishop allowed for his own capture by Taliban soldiers to keep said courier in sight. Special Agent Bishop escaped from known Taliban prison in the eastern Pakistani town of Multan with said courier and turned him over to CIA field officer Martin Young. Suspected payment was obtained by Special Agent Bishop but nuclear materials were not found nor obtained.

Kyle Bishop

"I already know this. Why are you giving me this, Donald?" Bishop said to himself as he finished reading the first page of documents. He thumbed through the documents, looking for something that he did not already know. One document heading stood out, and Bishop began reading.

<u>*Classified*</u>   *15 March 1991*

SUBJECT: Special Agent Xavier Charnov Involved In Unsanctioned Assassinations

Reporting Agent Thomas Vrbale submits further evidence that Special Agent Xavier Charnov was involved in unsanctioned assassination of Lt. Gen. Javier Espinoza of the Cuban Revolutionary Armed Forces. Such assassinations of said military official or any CRAF official had not been approved. It has become clear that Special Agent Charnov is no longer mentally stable enough to fulfill job responsibilities that are required of an agent.

Thomas Vrable

"So Xavier did work for us," Bishop said. "Son of a bitch!"

<u>*Classified*</u>   *15 December 1987*

SUBJECT: Special Agent Xavier Charnov Possibly Involved In Espionage Against United States

Reporting Special Agent Thomas Vrable submits that evidence suggests that Special Agent Xavier Charnov may be involved in the selling and trading of United States CIA files to unknown buyer or buyers. Further extensive research, into Special Agent Charnov's background showed evidence of Special Agent Charnovs personal involvement with female Soviet KGB agent.

Thomas Vrable

<u>*Classified*</u>   *26 January 1988*

SUBJECT: Special Agent Xavier Charnov Possibly Involved In Death Of Agent Thomas Vrable

Reporting Special Agent Jonathan Striker of the United States Army submits that Agent Thomas Vrable was found dead in a hotel room in Miami, Florida. As of June 1987, Agent Vrable reported to administrators that Special Agent Xavier Charnov had been exhibiting aggressive and at times questionable interrogation tactics. Special Agent Charnov and Agent Vrable were working a joint investigation into possible Soviet Union arms deals to Iran. Investigation was to establish validity of previous report, and to identify major dealer brokering the deal. According to previous reports made by Agent Vrable, evidence suggested that Special Agent Charnov was possibly working with unknown individual or individuals to expedite arms deals. It is the summation of Special Agent Jonathan Striker that Special Agent Charnov murdered Agent Vrable for his knowledge of Special Agent Charnov's involvement of arms deals.

Jonathan Striker

<u>*Classified*</u>   *4 March 1989*

SUBJECT: Disappearance Of Special Agent Xavier Charnov

Reporting Special Agent Jonathan Striker of the United States Army submits that Special Agent Xavier Charnov has disappeared. Special Agent Striker attempted to bring Special Agent Charnov into custody for questioning and when Special Agent Striker went to Special Agent Charnov's residence he found that Special Agent Charnov had left without evidence of next location. Special Agent Striker reports that furniture and most belongings were still in Special Agent Charnov's residence; however all of Special

Agent Charnov's clothes were missing, suggesting that said agent was no longer residing there.

Jonathan Striker

<u>*Classified*</u>   *15 August 1993*

SUBJECT: All Attempts To Locate Former Special Agent Xavier Charnov Have Turned Cold

Reporting Special Agent Jonathan Striker of the United States Army submits that all attempts to locate former Special Agent Charnov have failed. Every available resource to locate said agent has resulted in dead-ends. It is the summation of Special Agent Jonathan Striker that Special Agent Charnov has turned on the United States government and should be considered a high threat to national security.

Jonathan Striker

<u>*Classified*</u>   *7 February 1996*

SUBJECT: FBI Investigation Of Chicago Mafia May Show Evidence Of Special Agent Xavier Charnov's Whereabouts

Reporting Special Agent Jonathan Striker of the United States Army submits that he was informed by Agent Gregory Brown of the FBI that evidence in their investigation of a Chicago mafia syndicate shows that former Special Agent Xavier Charnov was working for said mafia as an enforcer for hire.

Jonathan Striker

Bishop finished reading the documents and drove back to Mary's apartment in Baltimore. When he arrived at the apartment complex he noticed an unfamiliar car parked in Mary's parking space. He got out and approached the car to examine it. It was a green, very unassuming Toyota Camry; nothing about the car stood out. The inside of the car was clean and completely empty.

Bishop walked to the top of the stairs to Mary's apartment and turned the corner. WACK!!! Bishop momentarily felt a hard strike to the back of his head before passing out. He never saw a thing.

When he came to, Bishop was still lying face down at the top of the stairs. He staggered as he attempted to get to his feet. His vision was slightly blurred and he was feeling nauseous, he was definitely suffering from a concussion. He searched his pockets for his keys and in doing so, he noticed that his wallet was missing. "I just got mugged," he thought to himself. He pulled out his keys and opened the door. The concussion he was suffering was really affecting him because he failed to notice that the door was already unlocked.

As he opened the door, he called out "Mary?!" The door opened about halfway and stopped abruptly. Bishop pushed it some more and was suddenly blown back against the wall by an explosion.

"I'm sorry sir," the fire fighter said. "I'm sorry." Bishop was sitting on a gurney out on the sidewalk in front of the apartment complex while the firefighters made sure that the apartment was safe enough for investigators to enter. Bishop didn't need the confirmation from the fire fighter; he knew Mary was dead.

Bishop had been sitting there on the gurney for well over an hour in an almost catatonic state. When Paul Donald finally showed up, he found Bishop sitting there staring up at the dry-wall laden debris that was sprawled out on the second floor hallway and staircase. "Bishop? . . . Bishop!," Donald said.

"My baby, have they found my baby?" Bishop said as he stared off into space.

"I'm so sorry, Bishop," Donald said.

"My baby, have they found my baby?" Bishop said again. He sounded robotic and completely detached from everything around him.

"I'll find out," Donald said.

Donald's regrettable attempt to find out if Bishop's son had survived proved to be futile. When he came back, he found Bishop up on his feet. Before Donald could offer any more of his condolences, Bishop informed him that he would see him in the morning. "Tomorrow, let's figure out what we're going to do about Carter and Xavier."

Donald didn't know what to say to him. He could tell that Bishop was completely and totally detached from reality. Paul Donald wasn't a psycho-analyst, but it didn't take one to figure out that Bishop was certainly in denial of what had occurred.

"We've got a good team of people working on it. Why don't you take some time and come back when you're ready?" Donald said.

"What do you mean? I'm ready now," Bishop replied.

"Bishop, do you understand . . . what happened here?" Donald asked.

Bishop lunged forward and grabbed Donald by his tie. He stared into Donald's eyes with a crazed fiery glare, he looked as though he was going to rip Donald's head off, but instead he just stared at him for a few moments. Bishop finally calmed down a little and said, "Just figure out where I need to go."

CHAPTER 14

REVELATION

It only took a little over forty-eight hours for Donald and his team of analysts to positively identify Jefferson Carter, who had been hiding in plain sight at his brother's home in Rome. When Donald had decided that the surveillance photos did indeed show Jefferson Carter in Rome, he immediately called Bishop.

"We confirmed it, Jefferson Carter is in Rome."

"When do I leave?" Bishop asked. His burning desire to avenge his family's death was masked by a somber, defeated demeanor.

"I can get you and a team on a plane in two hours," Donald said. "Bishop, I can't honestly imagine to try and relate to what you're going through right now, but as your friend, I have to say that I think this is a bad idea. You should let our team take care of Carter. You need to take some time off and grieve."

"How about you just worry about doing your job and getting me on a plane to wherever I need to go?" Bishop said. "And I'm going alone, I don't need a babysitter."

Bishop didn't care what Paul Donald had to say. Bishop was clearly no longer driven by doing what was right, he was now driven by anger, rage . . . vengeance. From this point on, Paul Donald knew that "by the book" procedure was probably not going to apply to Bishop.

At the airport, Bishop was met by three CIA agents sent by Donald. He didn't even get twenty feet to them before he addressed them. "You can all turn around and go home," he said. "There's nothing you can do here."

Bishop started walking forward as if no-one was even in front of him. One of the men stepped forward, put his hand out against Bishop's chest and said, "Mr. Bishop, we've been instructed to come with you. Our orders come directly from Langley. If you have a problem with that, then take it up with the guys with the higher paychecks." The agent started walking right past him when Bishop wrapped an arm around his neck and pulled out his gun, pointing it at the agent's head.

"Like I said, you can all go home," he said. Bishop then struck the agent across the back of the head and pointed his gun at the other agents. While the one agent stood there hunched over, holding his head in pain, the other agents just watched Bishop walk away without even attempting to say or do anything to stop him.

Bishop boarded the private jet at Andrews Air Force Base and sat down in his seat. He only brought with him a carry-on bag that contained a change of clothes, his journal, and his gun. After he settled into his seat, Bishop reached into his bag and pulled out his journal.

June 16

> *Can life really be this unfair? Can God really be this trying, this mean, this cold, this apathetic? Is there a God? Is there? Are you listening to me? Are you paying attention to what I'm saying? Do you care?*

The scenery through the window was black, empty and seemingly infinite. Bishop couldn't help looking out the window and think about how seemingly empty his own life was. Fame, fortune or even the idea of saving the world couldn't fill the hole in Bishop. He needed one thing and one thing only to make him happy again . . .

Bishop landed in Italy and when he got there, all he wanted to do was kill. It was nearly 2:00 a.m. when Bishop arrived in Italy. The intelligence reports given to Bishop indicated that Carter's mansion was in Naples. The mansion's original structure was built in the 8th century. Over the near twelve hundred years of the building's history, it had been modified and expanded countless times.

Bishop arrived at the estate under the cover of darkness, armed with his pistol and a cold, callous and unrelenting attitude. The mansion was not particularly well-garrisoned; just a small white wall surrounded the home, a seemingly decorative feature, rather than a protective measure. He approached the front door and as he got nearer, he found a guard sitting in a chair next to the entrance. Bishop could tell that the man was asleep, so he quietly walked up to him, covered his mouth with his left hand and grasped his forehead with his right, and violently broke the guard's neck.

He entered the house through the front door and quietly searched the rooms. He came to a hallway and found himself toe to toe with another guard. There was no time for being stealth, so he stood there facing the guard in a classic old west gun duel. The guard had his Springfield semi-automatic pistol holstered under his left arm. Bishop had his Glock 19 hand gun in his back waistband.

They stared each other down, their egos keeping them at bay, waiting for the other to make a move. Finally, the sound of a pistol being cocked froze Bishop. He didn't hear the third guard sneak up behind him. Bishop slowly reached for his gun and cautiously removed it from his waistband, dropped it on the floor and began to raise his hands. Before he got his palms above his head, Bishop reached back and grabbed the pistol pointed at the back of his head. In one swift motion, he spun around, causing the guard to fire a shot. As Bishop spun, he grabbed the guard's neck and snapped it.

Assessing the situation, Bishop could see that the guard's single shot struck and killed his comrade. With the gunshot blaring through the house, Bishop picked up his gun and hurried into the last room. There he found Jefferson Carter standing in the middle of the room, confused and scared.

"Trudeaux?" Carter said.

"Where's your brother?" Bishop asked. Jefferson Carter still remembered Bishop as Trudeaux from when he visited him in Baton Rouge.

"My brother? I don't know what you're talking about," Carter said.

Bishop pistol whipped him across the face. Carter wiped away blood that started spilling from his nose, only to have another large stream pour down over his lips and off of his chin. "Would you care to rethink that?" he asked.

"He's not here. He's at his home in Rome," he said begrudgingly. "Jesus, you broke my nose."

"Start talking. Tell me what's going on. What's your involvement with Paul Jenkins? Why are you still alive?"

"Jenkins was helping me to create my fuel cell. I'm a businessman. I found a way to revolutionize the world's dependency on fossil fuels. Jenkins helped me obtain the nuclear materials needed to ignite the source. We were partners. This technology was going to make Edison's light bulb look like an insignificant, distant memory and Jenkins knew the risks involved."

"What do you mean?" Bishop asked.

"I know you've already taken care of Jenkins, just like he said you would," Carter replied. Bishop was perplexed. Carter could tell by the look on his face that he didn't know what he was talking about. "You don't know, do you?"

"What do you mean?" he asked again. "Who else is involved?"

Carter knew that Bishop was not going to show him any mercy. He knew that death was imminent, so he figured, why die with a guilty conscience? "Jenkins was just a facilitator for the uranium; he wasn't really a main player in any of this. He said that once Jenkins did his part, he'd get rid of him and we would split the profits fifty-fifty. A couple of months ago, he told me that someone was getting too close, I now assume that person was you."

"Who are you talking about?" Bishop demanded as he cocked his gun.

"You really don't get it, do you? Donald . . . Paul Donald," he said. Bishop's heart sank. "He was the one who introduced me to Jenkins. Apparently, the U.S. government doesn't pay its servants very well. Donald and I were going to ride this new fuel technology all the way to the bank, selling the technology to the highest bidder. The applications and implications are limitless. In the hands of a legitimate Fortune 500 company, it could revolutionize the fossil fuel market. In the hands of dictator or lunatic religious faction, it could be the weapon to level the playing field for any second or third world country with a grudge against the United States. When you started getting too close to this, he helped me fake my own death. As far as Jenkins is concerned, Donald knew you would kill him before he could tip you off to Donald's involvement."

"Well I guess we both trusted the wrong person, because not only did he send me to kill Jenkins, he sent me to kill you as well," Bishop said. BANG! . . . BANG! BANG! Bishop fired two shots into Carter's chest and one between his eyes.

Thoughts, revelations, realizations all bombarded Bishop's mind. "Paul Donald, Jenkins, and Xavier all knew each other from the military. Donald wanted me to clean up the loose ends so that he wouldn't be exposed. He counted on me to kill Jenkins and Carter without me finding out about any of this. He used me to clean up his mess." Of all the sinister motives known to man: lust, vengeance, power, . . . Paul Donald's greed was every bit as simple and rational of a motive.

Bishop made his way back to the airport and boarded his private plane back to the States. The eight hour flight seemed to pass by in no time at all. He wrote in his journal all most the entire time and I suppose when you're mind is so incredibly focused on something so important, everything around you just doesn't exist.

June 17

> *Today I found that there is no God, in the conventional sense. There is no one great benevolent, altruistic God. How can someone or something supposedly care so much about me, and then allow innocent people that I love to be taken away from me so quickly . . . so prematurely?*

It was just past sunrise when the plane touched down at Andrews Air Force Base. He didn't even say goodbye or thank you to his pilot as he exited the plane. When Bishop arrived back in Baltimore, he didn't know what to do. He thought he knew what he was going to do, but when he actually got back home, the realization of killing Paul Donald was more difficult of a task than he had anticipated. He got off the plane and checked his phone for messages. His manager had tried calling him all night, leaving Bishop six voice mails and eight text messages.

"Bishop, we need to talk about some promotional ads for the album. Also, the label has been calling me, asking me when Fighter was going to get back into the studio for another album. Call me back when you get this." He knew his manager was an early riser, so he had no reservations calling him that early.

"Hey, it's Bishop . . . I just got your messages. What's up?" The tone in his voice was less than enthusiastic. It's not that Bishop wasn't happy or disinterested with being in Fighter, he just clearly had other things on weighing on his mind.

"Yeah, thanks for calling me back. I need to talk to you about getting into the studio. The record label is breathing down my neck, asking 'When is the next Fighter album coming out? When are they going to release new material?' I swear, all they care about is making money."

"Actually, I do have a some things down on paper that I'd like to go over with the guys. So uh, I'll give them a call in the next few days and see if we can get together and try and work out some songs. How's that?"

"That'd be great, yeah. Just give me a call when you guys are putting some songs together and I'll talk to the label and get 'em off our back."

They exchanged pleasantries and finished their conversation. Bishop sat there for a moment in his car, staring off into the ether. He barely made it through the conversation, in fact, it had just ended and he couldn't even remember what they were talking about.

The emotions that Bishop was feeling on the drive to Paul Donald's house were eerily similar to how he felt after the explosion at Mary's house. The world just seemed to have no purpose or meaning for Bishop, except pain. He turned on the stereo and the first song that came on was one of his own, and not just any song, but one that he had written about Mary. "You gotta be kidding me," he said to himself.

Lights sped by Bishop's car, resembling that of spaceship in a movie going light speed. Finally, Bishop snapped out of the trance he was in and realized that he was going a hundred and five miles per hour. Fortunately for him, Paul Donald lived in an area away from most other people and there wasn't another car on the street. He saw the street up ahead and began to slow down.

From the outside of the house alone, you could tell that Paul Donald had done well for himself financially. A modern, two story, four thousand square foot home built on three acres of colonial era land, complete with a small slave quarter about a hundred yards from the house that Donald had converted into a tool shed.

Chapter 15

Harsh Reality

The faint, muffled sound of glass breaking could be heard throughout the house. It didn't concern Bishop because he knew that Paul Donald wasn't home. He knew that Donald had left for the night to be at a banquet honoring a colleague of Donald's. Since the banquet (which started at 7:00) was in D.C., some thirty miles away from Donald's home, Bishop was not at all concerned with him showing up anytime soon.

Bishop knew that getting into Donald's office at the CIA complex in Langley was next to impossible, so he decided on checking out his home first. He was looking for anything he could use, anything that could incriminate Donald, linking him to any of the missions he ordered Bishop to take on and especially any evidence showing Donald's connection to Jefferson Carter and Xavier.

It wasn't long before Bishop found what he was looking for, or so he thought. In the master bathroom, Bishop stood in the middle of the room staring into the mirror. For nearly five straight minutes, Bishop stood there motionless, just staring into his own abyss, trying to find a soul.

Finally, after his stare-down with his own conscience, Bishop found the concealed latch holding the mirror against the wall. He lifted the latch and discovered a small safe with a digital combination lock. A black on black digital panel with raised numbers on the key pad spanning zero to twenty, separated Bishop from whatever evidence linking Paul Donald to Jefferson Carter and hopefully Xavier.

"All right, now how do I open you?" he said to himself. It struck him like a bolt of electricity. The conversation Bishop and Donald had nearly five years ago suddenly popped into his head.

"Another year passed," he told Bishop. "I can't believe it's been fifteen years ago today. Jesus, why do we remember the bad times so vividly and struggle to remember the good ones? People can be so morbid and macabre without even realizing it. It seems like it's in our genetic fibers. November 15, 1985, the day Sarah died . . . my wife. That day, I died. That may seem foreign to you. You may have no idea what I'm talking about but . . ." He didn't finish his sentence. He just glared off into thought.

"Eleven . . ." Bishop said to himself as he entered the numbers. "Fifteen . . . Eight . . . Five." After pressing the numbers, his finger hovered over the enter key. For a moment, he hesitated. "ENTER."

The safe made a "click" sound and Bishop grasped the handle. He opened the safe and found exactly what he feared he would find . . . nothing. The safe was empty.

"Bishop, what are you doing here?" The voice of Paul Donald startled Bishop. He had snuck up behind him as he was opening up the lock-box.

Bishop just stood there and shook his head in disgust. "How could you kill my child, my son? Mary . . . how could you kill Mary?" The ivory colored marble floor seemed to roll and the fine lines between tiles seemed to expand and contract. The culmination of all the shock and disbelief, anger and disappointment all hit him at once and caused a sort of sorrow laden vertigo.

"Bishop, I swear to you, I had nothing to do . . ."

"DON'T YOU LIE TO ME! Don't you lie to me, Paul," Bishop responded.

"Striker or Jenkins, which one was it? Which one told you that I was the spy? They're lying to you Bishop. I'm not the spy . . . they're lying."

The room started spinning again uncontrollably, tiles oscillating and grout lines expanding and contrasting. If Bishop wasn't left with the small grasp of reality that he had, he may have been permanently lost in that room.

Bishop could hear Paul Donald talking, but nothing was coherent. His words sounded like whale calls deep under the ocean. Donald began to dial a number on his phone and Bishop instantly snapped back to reality.

Armed with the less than foreboding toilet brush, Bishop swatted the phone from Donald's hand before he could finish dialing. He sprung to his feet and lunged at Donald. The two struggled, exchanging short elbow and knee shots to whatever unprotected spot they found.

A flailing arm, one that to an onlooker would not be able to correctly identify its owner, crashed into the mirror. As the two men grappled and fought, blood sprayed across the room like a lawn sprinkler.

Finally, after the struggle had ended, Paul Donald slowly stood up. His eyes were gazing into Bishop, who was still laying on his back on the blood covered floor. A stream of blood fell from Donald's mouth and off of his chin. A six inch broken shard of glass from the mirror was wedged into his back. It went in far enough to slice through his heart and puncture his lung. It took seconds for the lung to fill with blood. He dropped to the floor in front of Bishop. Bishop turned over on his side and stared at Donald and the shard of glass sticking into his chest.

His friend. His mentor. His enemy. Most people would have been overcome by emotion, but Bishop was feeling calm. The vertigo was gone, as was any and all emotions. He simply felt nothing. He was nothing. Not a discernible characteristic of human emotion remained.

After a few minutes, Bishop gathered himself and stood up. He spent the next twenty minutes rummaging through papers that Donald had kept away in a desk in his office. Paper after paper, invoice after invoice, letter after letter, Bishop thoroughly looked for anything linking Paul Donald to Xavier or Jefferson Carter. Finally, he found bank statements from Vatican City.

$85,000 deposit. $70,000 deposit. $44,000 deposit. $115,000 deposit. Page after page he read, all deposits of tens and hundreds of thousands of dollars and all coming from the same bank account . . .

Jonathon Striker. "Striker, Striker, Striker . . . where do I know that name?" he thought to himself.

He left the house and started driving. It was already in the late night/early morning phase. Pitch black, without a single soul roaming the street. Not even the sound or headlight glare of a single automobile was on the street.

"Mopped the floor, picked up all the broken glass, removed the rest of the broken mirror, wiped down the safe, the door knobs, the counter . . . vacuumed the carpet . . . What am I forgetting?" Bishop thought to himself as he finished cleaning.

After he left the house, the thought was still pounding in his brain. "Where do I know that name? Jonathan Striker? How is he connected to Donald? What does he have to do with Jefferson Carter? More importantly, what's his connection to Xavier?"

It dawned him, Donald and Striker were friends back in the Army and Xavier served under Donald. Striker was the first one in charge of Falcon, and he saw the potential financial benefits from carrying out those missions. Then when that ended, he decided to continue on his own, recruiting his own soldiers carrying out his own profitable missions. Xavier must have been one of those soldiers.

Now knowing the who and the why, only answered half of Bishop's questions. He still had no idea where to find Xavier. He was quite sure that it would take him a long time to find him, unless he got lucky some how, and that was okay with Bishop. He was prepared to spend the rest of his life trying and if nothing else waiting to find Xavier. Resigning to the fact that he might never find Xavier was not an option to Bishop; taking a lifetime however, was.

More than a month had passed since Bishop (took care of Donald) and he was still just as lost as ever. He'd go out for a run almost every day just to hopefully clear his head, even if it were just for an hour or so. After a while, he realized that he was running to get away. For miles and miles he ran, not knowing where he was going and before too long, he had forgotten where he was coming from. The distance he had put between himself and whatever it was he was running from, seemed to stand idle. No matter where he went, what he did, who he tried to be, he realized that the ominous thing that he was running from, was himself.

One day, after he returned back from a run, he checked his voicemail and got a message from James, Fighter's guitar player. "Hey man, it's James. Give me a call when you get this. The guys and I just wanted to check on you and see how you were doing. We've been writing some music and wanted to run it past you. Anyway, I hope you're doing alright. Give me a call when you can. Alright man, talk to ya later."

He called him up and they talked for an hour. Bishop agreed to meet up with them at the studio where they recorded their last album. They spent three weeks, on and off recording and fine tuning what would be Fighter's third, and according to them, their best album.

They concluded the album and started talking about a tour schedule. Bishop was eager to get away. He wanted . . . needed to go anywhere that didn't remind him of Mary. The band talked about places they've yet gone to . . . Australia, New Zealand, Philippines, and about a dozen other countries on the far side of the world.

The tour started off without a hitch. They began their first four or five shows by playing five new songs. Bishop, being a music fan and former avid concert goer himself, knew that the majority of concert fans didn't want to hear mostly new music. The majority of concert goers wanted to hear songs they knew. They wanted to hear the hits. However, since Bishop became a professional musician, he learned that bands needed to play their new material in order to promote their new albums.

From October to March, Fighter toured all over the southern hemisphere and southeast Asia, which in those parts of the world, was summer time like in Australia or basically summer time year round for the countries on or very close to the Equator.

By the end of the tour, Bishop unfortunately was beginning to succumb to the same depression that he had been suffering from for the previous several months. The same thoughts were constantly beating him down. "Why would god do this to me? How could there be a caring God, a God that cares about me or what happens to me?"

Bishop, without telling any of his band mates or friends, made the decision to leave. He wasn't sure where he was going or how long he would be gone or if he was even coming back, but he knew that if he didn't get away, he would go crazy. He went home, packed two bags with casual clothes, tooth brush, toothpaste, and his wallet . . . and that was it. Anything else that he may need, he decided that he would just buy along the way.

The nearest public transit center was the train station. It was so late in the evening that most of the trains weren't leaving until morning, but Bishop didn't care. He wanted to get out of town and didn't care where. He went to the ticket counter and looked at what his options were for departure. He saw, (11:40 p.m. New York, Penn Station) and bought a single one-way ticket.

Bishop walked out onto the train station platform. It was eleven-thirty at night and along the platform only a few lamps dimly illuminated the passenger waiting area. The train was in sight and Bishop turned around and faced the city that he had called home for the past several years. Though he could barely see any of it through the moonless night, he didn't need to. He knew there was nothing left for him there. As he turned back around to await the train, he heard a soft voice through the darkness.

"Kyle."

As he turned his head and squinted through the dark, he tried his hardest not to recognize the voice. He tried not to because he couldn't bare the anguish of remembering. He was so mentally scarred that he just wanted to be content with the prospect of denial of what had happened, but alas, there was still something inside of him that couldn't let him forget. "Mary?"

"Hello Kyle," she said.

He was dumbfounded, stupefied, in complete shock . . . and every other euphemism you could come up with.

"How . . . how is this possible? I thought you were dead," he said.

"Paul Donald . . . he sent someone to kill you. He told me that he had his reasons, but he wasn't a monster, so he spared mine and Sam's life. He took us to some farmhouse and had people watching us around the clock," she explained.

"I still don't get how you knew that I was here, or how you got out of there," Bishop said.

Mary began to chuckle in disbelief. "This morning, Sam and I were sitting in our bedroom that we were confined to and all of a sudden, I heard gunshots and shouting outside. The next thing I knew, the CIA came storming in and got us out of there. Some guy named Tyler said they've been watching us. He was the one who told me where you were, and that you were leaving."

"Oh my god, Tyler Harper. He wasn't kidding; they really have been watching us," Bishop said. "So what now?"

Mary stood there and shrugged her shoulders and smiled.

"I don't know. I know a great diner we could go to," she said . . .

ABOUT THE AUTHOR

Jim Togerson grew up in Northern California as a product of the eighties MTV generation. Early on, he was fascinated by the action movies, books, and comic books of the time. He reveled in the heroes who narrowly escaped a painful death and, more importantly, who were clever and cool. He developed a love for the writers who could make an adventurous story come to life, as well as a respect for writers who could paint an image of a hero that made the reader question what it really meant to be heroic.

Jim is now living in Southern California, enjoying the sunshine and conserving the water.

Printed in the United States
By Bookmasters